FALLOW

OTHER BOOKS FROM

JORDAN L. HAWK:

Hainted

<u>Whyborne & Griffin:</u>
Widdershins
Threshold
Stormhaven
Necropolis
Bloodline
Hoarfrost
Maelstrom
Fallow

<u>Hexworld</u>
"The 13th Hex" (prequel short story)
Hexbreaker
Hexmaker (forthcoming)

<u>Spirits:</u>
Restless Spirits
Dangerous Spirits

<u>SPECTR</u>
Hunter of Demons
Master of Ghouls
Reaper of Souls
Eater of Lives
Destroyer of Worlds
Summoner of Storms
Mocker of Ravens
Dancer of Death

<u>Short stories:</u>
Heart of the Dragon
After the Fall (in the *Allegories of the Tarot* anthology)
Eidolon (A Whyborne & Griffin short story)
Remnant, written with KJ Charles (A Whyborne & Griffin / Secret Casebook of Simon Feximal story)
Carousel (A Whyborne & Griffin short story)

FALLOW

(Whyborne & Griffin No. 8)

JORDAN L. HAWK

Widdershins always knows its own.
Welcome home.

CHAPTER 1

Whyborne

THE WIND STRENGTHENED from over the ocean, coiling around the slender figure standing atop a craggy rock. She might have been some barbaric sea goddess, dressed in nothing but golden jewelry and a skirt of knotted seaweed. Dark swirls marked her pearlescent skin like war paint, and the stinging tendrils of her hair writhed as the autumnal breeze grew into a gale.

I kept a grip on my hat to prevent it from flying off. Even though I stood well back from the water in an attempt to preserve my suit, dampness flecked my exposed skin. I licked my lips and tasted salt.

The wind died away, just as quickly as it had arisen. My twin sister let her arms fall and turned to me, mouth splitting into a grin and revealing rows of shark's teeth. "I told you I've been practicing."

I crossed the strand to her, my shoes sinking into the moist sand. "Well done," I said as she climbed down from the rock. "You're as good as I am at drawing power from the maelstrom now." Which was only natural, I supposed, given our relationship to the magical vortex lying beneath Widdershins.

"Better," she countered. Her tentacle hair flicked out in a sudden blur and sent my hat flying from my head.

"Persephone!" I snatched it up, brushing sand off the brim. "This is serious. Not a time for-for childish pranks. We're preparing for war, in case you've forgotten."

Two months ago, the Fideles cult had used the power of the maelstrom to send a sorcerous beacon through the veil separating our world and the Outside. They meant to summon back the ancient masters who had ruled the earth thousands of years ago, who had created the ketoi and the umbrae, and twisted the arcane lines to form the maelstrom.

We'd failed to stop them from sending the signal and beginning what they called the Restoration. Eventually the inhuman masters would return, and if we failed a second time...

It didn't bear contemplating. The ketoi and umbrae would either be killed or enslaved, and I doubted humanity would fare much better.

"It doesn't mean we can never laugh again," Griffin said as he approached, the light of his lantern gleaming off Persephone's sleek skin.

I folded my arms over my chest. "I didn't say that," I replied, trying to conceal my annoyance. Judging from the look on his face, I failed.

Griffin didn't understand. How could he? He didn't know the truth about the maelstrom.

About *me*.

Oh, he thought he did. He'd seen...something...during our battle against the Fideles cult in July. And of course he already knew about my ketoi blood.

But I couldn't tell him worst of it, the thing I'd realized when I briefly touched the consciousness of the maelstrom. The vortex beneath Widdershins wasn't just a feature of the landscape, like a river or mountain. It was magic, and alive in a way I didn't entirely understand. It wanted things and acted to get them.

Chiefly, it wanted not to be used by the masters upon their return. And Persephone and I were the keys to its plan, its attempt to touch and understand the world, to give it hands and eyes and hearts to work its will.

In the end, my sister and I were the ones responsible for preventing the return of the masters. The sheer weight of our obligation threatened to overwhelm me at times. I'd spent every waking moment searching for any way to halt the Restoration and the return of the masters.

"Did you see?" Persephone asked Griffin.

"I did." He meant it literally—Griffin had returned from our Alaskan expedition with shadowsight, the ability to perceive magic. "You burned like a candle when you pulled on the maelstrom. Just as your brother does."

Persephone grinned happily. I tightened my arms across my chest and hunched my shoulders forward slightly. I was used to being the only one Griffin described in such a way, and I wasn't certain I cared to share it, even with my sister.

He looked handsome tonight—well, he always did, but his new suit from Dryden & Sons complimented his figure nicely. The rust-colored vest in particular brought out the brown threads in his green eyes and the russet in his hair.

"What did the spell look like?" Persephone asked. She crouched on the sand, the fins on her arms jutting out awkwardly.

Griffin's eyes went slightly unfocused as he considered. "The glare from the arcane line running under the beach can make it hard to see," he said. "But it was as though you took a needle and thread, and punched them through the fabric of the world. Then you drew the cloth together, and the wind came."

Persephone frowned, an expression far less ferocious than her smile. "We don't sew cloth beneath the sea," she reminded him.

"Of course." He grimaced. "It wasn't the most accurate description anyway. Think of it as weaving a net, then, to catch the wind."

I drew out my pocket watch and was startled at the time. "We should leave. I have work in the morning, after all."

Persephone perked up slightly. "You will see Maggie there?"

"Of course. Miss Parkhurst is my secretary." They'd met during the awfulness in July and struck up something of a friendship.

Persephone detached a pouch at her waist. "Will you take this to her?" she asked, passing it to me without opening it.

Even through the knotted seaweed, I could sense its faint call. "A summoning stone?" I asked blankly. "What on earth for? I can't imagine any reason Miss Parkhurst would need to summon ketoi—"

"One never knows," Griffin interrupted. "Before we go, may I ask the two of you to try something?"

"Yes!" Persephone said hastily, rising to her feet.

I looked pointedly at my watch again, but they both ignored me. Griffin gestured in the direction of the rock, where Persephone had cast her spell. "Have you tried working a spell in tandem?"

"No," I replied slowly. "Why?"

"What would happen? Would it be more powerful, or…?"

I hadn't the slightest idea. My damnable cousins, Theo and Fiona Endicott, had performed sorcery together to raise a tidal wave in an attempt to destroy Widdershins, so I knew it was at least theoretically possible.

"Let's try!" Persephone said eagerly.

"All right, but I'm not climbing on that boulder," I said. "I haven't the shoes for it."

She looked disappointed, but followed me a bit further up the beach. The slow pulse of magic through the veins of the earth throbbed against the soles of my feet. "Here. We're still on the arcane line, so it will be easy for us to draw on the maelstrom."

"What should we do?"

I had only the vaguest idea. "Cast the spell at the same time, I suppose."

"Would touching help?" Griffin asked. He stood a short distance back. He'd once touched me while I pulled arcane power from the lines, an experience neither of us wanted to repeat. Its effects hadn't been permanent, but it had hurt him at the time, bursting capillaries in his eyes and sending him reeling into unconsciousness.

Human bodies weren't meant to touch such power directly. But the maelstrom had spent years changing probabilities, nudging the odds this way and that, until Persephone and I were born. Sorcerers of ketoi blood, who could channel the magic directly without harm.

Persephone took my hand. Her skin was cool and slick against mine, the points of her claws pressing lightly as our fingers twined together.

"We'll summon the wind again," I said. "On three."

She nodded, her expression determined. "One," she said.

I took a deep breath, centering myself. The world seemed to still around me.

"Two."

My awareness of the power beneath our feet sharpened.

"Three."

I reached for the magic, shaping it with my will. Arcane energy surged through our bodies, and the scars on my right arm burned. I *felt* my sister beside me, her breathing and heartbeat matching mine.

We touched the world, and the world responded.

Wind roared in from the open ocean, a wall of force that knocked me to the ground. An instant later, the ocean answered the sky with a roar of its own. A massive wave rushed into the cove, bursting over the strand and nearly reaching the cliff. It surged around me, the greedy, cold water seeking to drag me into the sea.

I let out a surprised shout, clawing at sand that washed away beneath my fingers as quickly as I could grasp it. Then the wave receded, leaving me soaked to the bone and covered in seaweed, my shoes filled with sand.

I rose to my feet and wiped ineffectually at my suit. My hat was gone, probably blown all the way to Boston on the wind we'd summoned. A fish flopped on the beach beside me. Persephone picked it up and tossed it back into the surf.

"Well," I said, turning to Griffin. "That was…oh."

He stood dripping wet from head to toe, his new suit soaked in seawater. A strand of seaweed clung to his hair, and his hat had joined mine somewhere a few counties over.

"Yes," he said, plucking sadly at his ruined vest. "It certainly was."

~ * ~

"I'm so sorry," I said yet again as Griffin unlocked the door to our home.

Our journey from the beach had been uncomfortable. It was impossible to remove all the sand from our shoes and clothes. Salt stiffened our suits and crusted our skin. Once back in Widdershins proper, we'd attempted to hire a cab, but the driver had taken one look at our sodden state and left us on the curb. For the first time, I found myself regretting the destruction of Griffin's motor car.

"Stop apologizing," Griffin said, holding the door open for me. Once inside, he locked it again, then began to peel off his coat. "It isn't as though you knew what would happen."

"What did happen?" I asked. "From your point of view, I mean."

Griffin bit his lip, his eyes going thoughtful. "It isn't easy to describe. Your spells…resonated? Overlay each other? I wonder if perhaps the spells the Endicotts and other sorcerers do together are handled in a different fashion. Each one contributing a piece to a more complex whole."

That made sense. "Judging from what I've read in the *Arcanorum* and other magical texts, you're probably right."

"Could you and Persephone learn to perform spells like that?"

"Of course," I said, more sharply than I intended.

"I don't mean to cast aspersions on your abilities, my dear." Griffin offered me a smile as he unbuttoned his salt-stained vest. "But from what little I know of the matter, you and Persephone aren't quite the same as other sorcerers. You learn spells, yes, but they're something of a crutch that you can discard after a while. When was the last time you had to draw a sigil to summon wind, or chant to make frost appear?"

"It's only a matter of will for everyone," I insisted. Griffin didn't look as if he believed me.

I didn't believe myself. But the conversation was getting too close to things I didn't want to discuss with anyone except Persephone.

It wasn't that I wished to keep secrets from the man I called husband. But if he knew the terrible truth I'd learned in July, when I touched the maelstrom and perceived the world as it did...

He'd be furious, and rightfully so.

"I *am* sorry about the suit," I said, hoping to distract him. "It was brand new, and it looked so fine on you."

By unspoken consent, we'd remained in the hallway to remove our ruined clothing. No sense scattering sand and dripping water through the house. He peeled off his trousers and stood clad only in his drawers. His eyes followed my movements as I did the same. "You appreciated how it looked, did you?" he asked, and I recognized the low note in his voice.

"Very much so." I stepped closer, and he rested his hands on my hips, just above the edge of my drawers. His fingers felt chilled against my skin.

A slow smile curled his lips. "In that case, it's a shame to have lost it so soon." His grip on me tightened. "You'll have to make it up to me, I think."

"However shall I do that?" I murmured.

"You can start on your knees."

I dropped to the floor eagerly. The outline of his cock was already visible against the soft cotton drawers, and I peeled them off his damp skin. Gooseflesh roughened the skin of his legs, and I ran my hands up his thighs, feeling the familiar interruption of the scar wrapped around the right. I leaned close and nuzzled the soft skin of the juncture between thigh and groin, and his member jerked in reaction. He smelled of salt and ocean water, of musk and the fading traces of sandalwood.

"My dear," he whispered, his fingers trailing through my unruly hair.

I took him in my mouth, tasting his desire through the film of salt the sea had left behind. My own cock ached, and I dropped my hand and palmed myself through the fabric of my drawers. Before I could draw it out, he said, "Not yet. I want you in my mouth."

His voice trembled on the words, and I sucked harder, closing my eyes. He leaned against the wall as I wrapped my arms around his hips, half supporting him even as I worked him with tongue and throat. He groaned and shivered, fingers going tight in my hair, before he stiffened. "Ival," he gasped, and I swallowed down everything he had to give me.

He sagged against the wall for a moment, his breathing harsh, his beautiful eyes closed. Then he sank to his knees beside me, pulling me close and kissing me deep. "I love you," he growled, then shoved me onto my back.

He stripped off my drawers and tossed them into the pile of our wet clothing. "Pull your knees up," he ordered, and I hurried to comply. He propped himself in between my legs, wetting a finger before wrapping his lips around my cock.

I clutched at the hall rug as he took me deep into the heat of his mouth. At the same time, his finger pressed in, seeking and finding just the right spot. After almost four years together, we knew one another with an intimacy I'd never imagined, and he put his knowledge to good use. I cried out softly, writhing on the carpet. Griffin moaned encouragement, and I opened eyes I didn't remember closing to watch him suck me. The sight undid me, and I shuddered as I spent into his throat.

I collapsed back against the hall floor. The boards creaked slightly as our marmalade cat, Saul, came to investigate. Griffin rose to his feet, a bit stiffly, and held out a hand to me.

"Did I make up for the suit?" I asked.

He grinned and kissed me again. "The vest, at least. You still owe me for the coat…each leg of the trousers…the tie…"

I snorted and returned his kiss. "Fiend."

"That's why you love me."

"I suppose it is."

We washed the salt from our skin, then retreated to Griffin's bed. We had our separate rooms, to maintain a polite fiction for the cleaning lady and anyone else who might venture into our home, but we never slept apart. He drifted off into contented sleep within minutes, but despite the late hour and my own weariness, I found myself wakeful.

Griffin was the center of my world, the one I'd do anything for, if only to make him as happy as he made me. I'd spent my life in aching loneliness before he'd come into it, turning my dull gray existence into one of color and light. I sometimes felt as though he'd brought me to life. Or at least wakened me from a deep sleep, like some character in a fairytale cursed to dream away the years until roused by a kiss.

So the knowledge I was responsible for every bad thing that had happened to him over the last four years, every moment of horror and terror, felt like a rock sitting atop my chest.

In the chaos of last July, my longtime rival Bradley Osborne had finally given into jealousy and revenge. Dark magic had allowed him to swap bodies with me, so that he might use my bloodline to harness the power of the maelstrom and send the signal through the veil to summon the masters back to our world.

His human body hadn't been meant to withstand such arcane power, and had been crumbling to pieces even as I fought my way to him. And there had been a moment, after I'd stabbed him in the chest, when I'd been…between. My consciousness outside of any flesh.

Rejoined, briefly, to the maelstrom which I now knew had spawned it.

I'd touched the arcane vortex before, trying to stop the tidal wave raised by the Endicotts. Even then, I'd sensed the magic was different. Unlike the power the dweller in the deeps had lent me, this magic *was* me, or I was it. And the odd thought had floated through my head that perhaps there'd never been a *me* at all.

I hadn't realized then just how right I was. Until July, when I'd perceived the world through the maelstrom once again. I'd seen through the eyes of all the people it had drawn to Widdershins. The men and women, human and inhuman, it had collected over the long years of waiting for the masters' return.

Including Griffin.

And the worst part of it was, there were others whose minds had been touched by the umbrae. The maelstrom might have collected someone else. But it had chosen to bring Griffin into this horror.

I tightened my arm around his waist, pressing my face into the back of his neck. If not for the maelstrom, if not for me, he might have lived his life with only a single encounter with the otherworldly. After leaving the Pinkertons—or, rather, being locked away in an insane asylum and cast out from their ranks—he might have started his own business anywhere. New York, Boston, Kansas City; all far more likely places for a private detective than Widdershins.

But the maelstrom, somehow, sensed him. And in its blind, inhuman desire, it had nudged him at just the right moment, caused him to look down at precisely the right newspaper article when his father had asked him where he meant to go. At the time, the papers had been full of the great discovery made by Dr. Christine Putnam in Egypt, and of the journey of the mummy of Pharaoh Nephren-ka to the museum in Widdershins. So Griffin had, on a whim and with the name of the town laid out before him, decided to come here.

Just the tiniest push, the smallest alteration of chance. The pebble starting the avalanche.

Instead of spending the last four years in no more than the ordinary danger surrounding his profession, Griffin had found himself embroiled in magic and horror. We'd fought sorcerers and cultists, spoken to monsters beneath the mountains of Alaska, and fled for our lives through the wastes of Egypt. Griffin had bled and wept and suffered...and all because of me.

I could only pray he never found out.

CHAPTER 2

Whyborne

THE NEXT MORNING, I sat at my desk, the Wisborg Codex in front of me. Its open pages were carefully shielded by a host of other books stacked in front of it. Since the codex had already been stolen from my office once, the director would be furious if he knew Mr. Quinn had allowed me to remove it from the library again. As unnerving as I found him, the head librarian was a staunch ally, and I had no desire to get either of us in trouble.

The codex was encoded in cipher, and I'd hoped to find some key to unlocking it amidst Bradley's things. But discreet searches of his home and old office had revealed nothing.

I knew some of what the codex contained, if only because of what the Fideles had been able to accomplish after stealing it. Some part of it contained instructions for building and sending the beacon to signal the masters. Presumably it also gave instructions on what the Fideles referred to as the Restoration, which would prepare the world for the masters' rule.

If only I could tell what exactly the Restoration entailed, I might have some chance at stopping it. Or possibly even prevent the masters from returning to the world they'd abandoned so long ago.

There came a soft knock at my door. "A letter for you, Dr. Whyborne," said my secretary, Miss Parkhurst.

I sat back in my chair, wincing as my back popped audibly. "Thank you," I said, taking the letter from her. I didn't recognize the sender's name, although I was vaguely relieved to find it addressed to "Dr. P.E. Whyborne" and not "Widdershins."

My correspondence had gotten rather odd of late.

"Would you care for some coffee?" Miss Parkhurst asked with a gesture at my empty cup.

"Yes, thank you." I started to hand her the cup, then I recalled Persephone's gift. "Oh, wait—I have something for you."

An uncertain look crossed her face. "You have something...for me?" she asked, sounding oddly torn.

Why, I couldn't imagine. Miss Parkhurst was a wonderful secretary, but I occasionally found myself baffled by her. Of course, that was true of people in general. I sometimes envied the ease with which Griffin moved through society, always knowing what to say, what was expected of him.

"My sister asked me to give you this," I said, reaching into my desk.

"Persephone—that is, Miss Whyborne?" For some reason, her cheeks turned bright pink.

At my request, Griffin had replaced the wrapping of seaweed with one of silk. "It's a summoning stone," I explained as I passed it to her. "It—no! Don't unwrap it!"

Miss Parkhurst hastily folded the cloth tight, her face going even redder. I could feel a blush of my own staining my cheeks. "I'm sorry —forgive me for my rudeness," I said. "I should have warned you before handing it over." I took a deep breath and reminded myself that she knew Persephone was my sister. There was no reason to be embarrassed about my ancestry. "As I said, it's a summoning stone. In particular, it summons ketoi...or those of us with their blood. The silk keeps its call muted, but if you wouldn't mind not exposing it in my presence..."

"Oh!" She blushed even more furiously. "Of course."

"I've no idea why Persephone thought you would need one," I went on, trying to steer the conversation to any other topic. "I can't imagine why you would ever want to contact the ketoi."

"N-no," she agreed, the color still burning in her cheeks.

"But if you do, go to a secluded beach and throw it into the waves. They'll come. Persephone herself most likely, although our mother might answer instead."

The color drained from Miss Parkhurst's face. Was she quite all right? "Mrs. Whyborne?"

I doubted mother would care for the name any longer, but I'd already exposed poor Miss Parkhurst to enough of my family's eccentricities for one day. "Don't be frightened of her," I said. "Or any of the ketoi. They won't harm you, despite their savage appearance."

"I think they're beautiful," Miss Parkhurst said. Then her eyes widened sharply. "I—that is—I'll just get your coffee."

I stared after her, mystified, as she fled my office. Was it my imagination, or was my correspondence not the only thing growing odder?

With a sigh, I took out my letter opener and slit the envelope. The letter inside was hastily scrawled on cheap stationery bearing the monogram and address of a hotel in Topeka, Kansas.

Dr. Whyborne,

Forgive me for the imposition, but I must meet with you as soon as possible. I have information of great interest to yourself, which I cannot entrust to a letter. Allow me only to say that Reverend Scarrow is—or should I say was—a mutual friend. I fear his attempt to warn you about the Fideles came to the attention of the wrong people.

Oh no. In truth, I'd been concerned for Scarrow already. He'd sent me a telegram in July, with the promise of a longer letter to follow. That letter had never come, and I'd received no answer to those I sent him. But a part of me hoped there had simply been some interruption of the mail, or even that he'd been distracted by some concern of his own.

The Fideles will no doubt wish to end me as well, to prevent me from informing you of their plans. Hence, I must speak with you immediately. I will come to the Nathaniel R. Ladysmith Museum at 5:00 pm on Friday, September 27. Forgive me for granting you so little warning, but I'm sure you appreciate my urgency.

Sincerely,

Ralph Delancey

PS: Rumor has linked your name with that of Mr. Griffin Flaherty, formerly of Kansas. I believe some of what I have to say will be of interest to him as well.

CHAPTER 3

Griffin

I STARED AT Whyborne's note and barely suppressed the urge to tear it up and throw it into the trash.

This was not how the evening was meant to go. We weren't meant to be meeting some sorcerer, who might or might not be up to any good. I had made plans, curse it.

Ever since the battle against the Fideles in July, Whyborne's mood had grown increasingly morose. His tendency to work long hours became even more marked; the nights and weekends were spent with a book in his lap as he feverishly attempted to decipher the Wisborg Codex. And if not the codex, then his attention was entirely focused on Persephone and her mastery of the arcane arts.

And failing that, he paced about Widdershins like a soldier on guard duty. He'd badgered his father into paying to repair all the broken windows resulting from Bradley's activation of the arcane lines. Winter was coming, as Whyborne pointed out, and the poor shouldn't have to suffer the cold because of Bradley. Although I applauded his efforts, he seemed to feel it his personal responsibility to check every replacement, and send angry letters to the contractors Niles hired when he felt they weren't working quickly enough.

With so much occupying him, I'd started feeling a bit neglected, churlish though I knew the impulse to be. Last night had been the first time we'd made love in a fortnight.

In truth, though, I worried more for Ival than for me. The way he'd snapped at Persephone, when she indulged in a bit of horse play and knocked off his hat, reminded me how long it had been since I heard his laugh.

So I'd made plans for tonight as a surprise for him. Reservations for two at Le Calmar and a pair of tickets to the theater would ensure a pleasant evening, and keep his mind off of the masters, sorcery, and every other thing weighing down his spirits. We would enjoy a pleasant evening out, and when we came home I'd make love to him until his busy mind calmed and he could think of nothing else.

Except, of course, this blasted fellow Delancey meant to spoil those plans.

I put away the more formal suit I'd taken out in anticipation of an evening on the town, and replaced it with my everyday clothing. Shortly before five o'clock, I left the house and strolled down Water Street to catch the electric trolley to the museum. If only my poor Oldsmobile had survived. I'd barely had the chance to familiarize myself with driving it, before Bradley Osborne set fire to the gas tank. I'd already begun saving for another, but it would be some time before I could afford a replacement.

I could ask Niles for a loan, of course. But just the thought of Whyborne's reaction made me wince. Father and son might have put a patch on their relationship, but any mention of Niles's fortune was the surest way to make Ival's worst suspicions come to the fore.

I descended from the trolley near the museum and made my way up the familiar steps. The elderly ticket taker knew me well by now and merely lifted his hand in greeting as I passed by. The museum was in the process of closing for the day, and visitors streamed out the doors, a few pausing to take one last look at the hadrosaur skeleton dominating the grand foyer. As I made my way to the staff door, it swung open, and Christine and Iskander emerged.

"—had best not be late," Christine was saying to her husband. "I'm starving."

"And who chose to work through lunch?" Iskander asked with a lift of one brow. Although his mother's Egyptian blood had shaped the bones of Iskander's face and given him his bronze skin, his accent was that of an educated Englishman. He and Christine had met on her first dig in Egypt, and he'd moved to Widdershins last year to be with her.

Christine waved his objection off. "Yes, yes. Oh, hello, Griffin. I suppose Whyborne told you some sorcerer fellow is on his way?"

"I'm afraid so, though he didn't go into detail."

"Neither did Mr. Delancey," Whyborne said, emerging from the staff door himself. He looked tired—but these days, he always looked tired. The delicate lines forming around his eyes and mouth seemed more noticeable, and shadows ringed his eyes from sleepless nights. He'd neglected to visit the barber recently, so his untamable hair jutted in wild spikes. "Other than it has something to do with the Fideles and whatever new awfulness they have planned. I'm sorry for dragging you into this, Griffin, but Delancey mentioned you by name."

I frowned. "Even if he hadn't, I hope you wouldn't consider meeting an unknown sorcerer without the rest of us."

His gaze evaded mine. "No, of course not."

Once we returned home, we were going to have a serious conversation about his odd moods as of late. Something was clearly bothering him, beyond the obvious.

"That must be the fellow," Iskander said with a nod in the direction of the museum entrance.

The man making his way across the foyer looked perfectly ordinary at first glance. He might have been a low level clerk at some business, his suit clean but of last year's cut, his hair conservatively trimmed. His skin was lightly tanned, however, as though he'd recently spent time outdoors. In his left hand he carried a simple valise.

But one look dispelled any thought that this might be an ordinary clerk or salesman. Magic left its mark, revealed in my shadowsight as a sort of unnatural gleam about the eyes.

"He's a sorcerer all right," I said, shifting so I could feel the weight of my revolver in my pocket. I'd brought it even though guns were seldom safe to handle around sorcerers. More useful was my sword cane, which I held loosely in my right hand.

Whyborne straightened his shoulders. "I suppose I ought to speak with him then."

"*We* ought to," I corrected him. "And we should begin out here, where we're at least in view of the guards. It may restrain him if he means us ill."

Whyborne nodded and led the way across the marble floor. The man slowed, his eyes flicking over us each in turn. "Dr. Whyborne," he said. "And this must be Mr. Flaherty, Mr. Barnett, and Dr. Putnam."

"It's Dr. Putnam-Barnett now, but yes," Christine said. "And if you know our names, you know Whyborne relies on us in these, er, matters."

Whyborne looked rather pained at her words. "Yes," he said heavily. "You said you wished to speak to me about the Fideles, Mr. Delancey. Why did you want Griffin involved?"

The small, discreet side door near the main doors opened. One of the security guards moved to talk to the man who stepped inside.

Delancey remained focused on Whyborne. "There are plans afoot of which you are ignorant," he said. "Forces moving to strike not just you, but this entire town."

Whyborne's frown deepened. "The Restoration Scarrow warned us about?"

"In part. You are sitting atop an incredibly potent source of power, Dr. Whyborne," he said, lowering his voice. "The Fideles were fools—they listened to your brother and Dr. Osborne, when they should have reached out to you as the Cabal did."

The man I'd noticed earlier had gained admittance and walked briskly toward us. Warning bells sounded in my mind, my instincts drawing my attention away from Delancey and to the newcomer. I opened my mouth to call out to him, but the words died on my lips, replaced by horror.

It was clear at a glance that something was deeply wrong with the man. Some sort of *corruption*—I had no other word for it—spread hideous gray hyphae across his features. As if something had taken root inside and grew like a horrible mold over his skin.

Bile stung the back of my throat at the sight, my stomach threatening to turn at the awful *wrongness*. "Dear God!"

"Whatever is the matter?" Iskander asked, looking from me to the corrupted man. In that moment, I realized two things.

First, the corruption was only visible to my shadowsight.

Second, the man had reached into his coat and drawn out a pistol.

~ * ~

I reacted on sheer instinct. We were out in the open, with no immediate cover, so I did the only thing I could and tackled

Whyborne.

We struck the museum floor at the same instant the gun fired. Warm blood hit the side of my face, and for a heart-stopping moment I thought Whyborne had been shot.

Delancey's lifeless body collapsed to the floor beside us.

I rolled off of Whyborne and to my feet. I'd lost my sword cane when I knocked him away from the assassin, so I reached into my coat and pulled out my revolver.

The man let his hand fall to his side, although he didn't let go of the gun. He stared straight ahead, blinking slowly, as though now that he'd shot Delancey, he had no will to do anything else.

"Drop the gun!" one of the security guards shouted.

"There's something wrong with him!" I yelled. I didn't want to touch him, not even to grab the gun away. The horrible, grayish-black filaments seemed to writhe and flex across the back of his hands and over his face—

His face.

Dear God. It couldn't be. But I *knew* those features, even though it had been fourteen years since I'd last seen them. Hadn't I beheld them every Sunday of my childhood at church, at picnics, at potlucks and community dances?

"Mr. Odell?" I asked, bewildered.

"Griffin Flaherty," he said. Then his face transformed into a snarl of rage, and he raised his gun a second time.

There came the crack of a pistol, echoing throughout the cavernous space. Odell collapsed in front of me, blood spreading across his chest. The museum guards rushed up with their weapons trained on him, but it was clear he was no longer a threat.

His breath rattled in his lungs, blood already filling them. I dropped to my knees beside him. "Mr. Odell? What's going on?"

His dimming gaze fixed on me. "You'll pay for what you did," he managed to say through the blood choking him. Then he drew one last, rattling breath and grew still.

Whyborne's hand came to rest on my shoulder. "Griffin? You know this man?"

I nodded. "Cotton Odell. I haven't seen him in...it must be fourteen years now." He'd been one of the men waiting for me at the depot, to make certain I got on the train that would take me out of Kansas. Out of the community where I'd grown up, the community where he was a respected man.

When I was a small child, he'd bought me penny candy from the barrel at the general store. When I was a youth, he'd always laughed and joked every time we'd see one another at picnics, or church, or in town to buy supplies.

But that day there had been no laughter, no jokes. Not even a smile. Nothing but cold judgment and disgust, for bending over the milking stool in the barn and letting the neighbor's son fuck me.

"You'll pay for what you did." Surely Odell hadn't meant that long-ago scandal.

"Is he from Chicago?" Whyborne asked.

"No. He's from my hometown." I licked dry lips. "From Fallow."

CHAPTER 4

Whyborne

"SO YOU KNEW this fellow, Griffin?" Christine asked.

We'd retreated to my office once the police finished questioning us. They'd taken away the bodies and Mr. Odell's pistol, but Iskander had the presence of mind to pretend Delancey's valise belonged to him, dropped in the confusion of the moment. Now he set it on my desk. Christine placed a bottle of whiskey she'd retrieved from her own office beside it.

Griffin shut the door behind him and leaned against it. He was in his shirtsleeves, his coat having been spattered with Delancey's blood. While he washed the blood off of his face, I'd retrieved his belongings from the pockets of his ruined coat, and found a pair of theater tickets for tonight.

No doubt he'd meant them as a surprise for me. Unfortunately, it wasn't the first time his romantic plans had been interrupted.

If Griffin had gone to live in some other city, he would surely have found some other man. One not constantly surrounded by madness and death. They'd manage something as simple as dinner and the theater without having to think twice about it.

"Mr. Odell," Griffin said. He stared at the floor, his arms folded over his chest. "Yes. He was from Fallow. He was a farmer. Well respected." His lips tightened slightly, as if at some memory.

"Fallow?" Iskander asked. "It seems an odd name for an agricultural town."

"It's shortened from 'Fallow Place,' I believe, which was just a mark on the early maps. There's a barren patch of earth, maybe ten or twelve acres, where nothing grows. No one knows why—even if you try to plant it, nothing will come up, no matter what you do. There are all sorts of stories about the devil emerging from hell there every night, or Indian ghosts, or what have you." A tiny smile flickered over his lips. "Benjamin Walter and I sat out there on a dare one night, when we were boys. We ended up scaring each other silly and ran all the way back to the house long before midnight."

I wanted to touch him, but the way he'd withdrawn into himself made me uncertain if it would be welcome. "And this Walter was the fellow who…er…"

"I was caught with, yes." Griffin shook his head. "And Mr. Odell was one of the men who made certain I was on the train for Chicago shortly after."

"No loss, then," Christine opined. She took a pull straight from the whiskey bottle before passing it to Griffin.

Iskander rubbed at his chin. "Surely Odell wasn't referring to that incident, when he shouted at you," he said to Griffin. "Did he have some other grudge?"

"None that I can imagine." Griffin took a drink from the bottle and offered it to me. I refrained, as did Iskander, so it returned to Christine. "It's been fourteen years since I laid eyes on the man. I've only returned to Fallow once since, when Pa took me home after… after the asylum." He swallowed heavily. "One or two other people saw me then, of course, but for the most part I kept to myself."

I tentatively touched the back of his hand. He cast me a grateful smile and linked his fingers with mine.

"Maybe it didn't have anything to do with the incident, then," Iskander said. "Odell must have been a member of the Fideles cult. Delancey said they wished him dead, and Odell was the assassin they sent. It was merely a coincidence that he and Griffin knew one another."

"Perhaps, but Delancey specifically asked for Griffin in his letter," I reminded them. "And he had just come from Kansas himself."

"None of this makes sense." Griffin shook his head. "Mr. Odell couldn't be a member of the cult! He was a farmer. A simple man—intelligent, but uneducated. And the...the *corruption* on him. In him." He shuddered.

I frowned. "Corruption? You said something was wrong with him. Your shadowsight revealed some spell, or...?"

"I'm actually not certain." Griffin sighed and took the bottle back from Christine. "It didn't look like a spell, though. I could see dark... roots, almost, under his skin. Like some sort of fungal hyphae spreading through him."

"How ghastly," Christine said. "Does that sound like any sorcery you've heard of, Whyborne?"

"No," I said. "Let's go through Delancey's valise—perhaps there will be some clue as to why he wanted to speak with Griffin as well as me."

As Christine was perched on my desk, she leaned over and opened the valise. A frown crossed her face as she peered inside. "What the devil?"

I released Griffin's hand and joined her. Inside the valise was a smooth sphere about the size of an orange, made from some sort of metal I didn't recognize at all.

I reached inside and pulled it out. The greenish-black metal revealed hidden bands of color when I turned it in my hands. A large hole appeared to have been burned or melted into it at some time in the distant past, revealing a hollow, featureless interior. Fresher scratches and a slight dint marred its exterior. There seemed to be some sort of ornamentation around its equator, and I felt a chill at the sight of the strange clusters of dots. "Oh my God. Christine?"

She snatched the sphere from me. Her dark eyes narrowed as she examined it carefully, her mouth drawing tighter and tighter as she did. "Blast," she said at last. "I'd have to compare it directly with the stele to be absolutely certain, of course, but..."

"But it's the same writing—if it is writing—as was on the stele and in the city of the umbrae," I finished grimly. "The city the masters built."

"Yes."

No wonder the Fideles were involved. Had they been hoping to get the sphere from Delancey, or just to keep him from showing it to me? "If only we could read the masters' script. What does it look like in your shadowsight, Griffin?"

"There's nothing to be seen," he said. "If there was ever any sort of magic associated with it, it faded away long ago."

Christine turned the sphere over in her hands again, examining it with a practiced eye. "There are bits of dirt clinging to the inside. As if it was buried, and someone tried to clean it once it was dug up. And look at this." She ran her finger over the edge of the hole in it. "Do you see what I do, Kander?"

An expression of unease crossed over his handsome face. "It almost looks as though the metal was burned through from the inside. But that isn't possible."

"I wouldn't dismiss anything as impossible when dealing with the works of the masters," I said. "Is there anything else in the valise? Some hint as to what the sphere is, or where it came from?"

Iskander peered inside, then shook his head. "No. I should have searched his pockets, but I didn't think to."

"None of us did," Griffin replied. "Perhaps—"

There came a sharp knock on the door at his back. We all jumped, and Christine hastily shoved the sphere into the valise.

Griffin opened the door cautiously. One of the museum guards stood in the hall, a policeman behind him. "Excuse me, Dr. Whyborne, Dr. Putnam-Barnett," the guard said. "This fellow here was looking for Dr. Whyborne."

"Of course," I said. "Did you have some more questions for us, officer?"

"Begging your pardon, Dr. Whyborne," the policeman said with a quick bob of his head. "But Detective Tilton sent me. He'd like to request your presence at…well, at the morgue, sir."

~ * ~

"Through here, if you please," said the attendant. We stood in the large front room of the city morgue, where unidentified bodies were laid out for viewing. As it was night, the place was closed to the public at the moment, and we were alone in the viewing area save for the attendant and a single body. I glanced at it—then quickly away. The poor fellow looked to have been in the water for some time, and the fish had done their grim work.

Dr. Greene, the medical examiner, awaited us in the autopsy

room, an expression almost of fear on his features. Detective Tilton lurked in the corner; he tipped his hat in greeting. "Thank you for coming at this late hour."

"Of course." I gestured to Christine. "I'm sure you recall Dr. Putnam-Barnett."

Tilton frowned and gave me a sharp look. "She should wait outside. This is no sight for a woman."

Christine drew herself up, eyes flashing. "If you believe this is the first dead body I've seen, you're quite mistaken. I assure you—"

"I take it this has something to do with the murder in the museum?" Griffin asked quickly. Distracted by the question, Tilton nodded.

"Dr. Greene, would you do the honors?" he asked.

Two bodies lay on the steel tables, each covered by a sheet. Dr. Greene approached one of them with visible reluctance. Given some of the things he'd no doubt seen, his fear and caution left me rather unsettled. "Mr. Delancey's body was normal in every respect for a man of his age," Dr. Greene said with the air of a man putting off something unpleasant. "Mr. Odell, on the other hand...well. See for yourself."

He pulled back the sheet to the corpse's waist. Odell lay still opened for inspection, his organs displayed to the air. The top of his skull rested beside his shoulder, leaving his brain exposed.

Nausea twisted my gut, and I swallowed convulsively. Thank God I hadn't eaten dinner. And what on earth was that noxious smell? Like a compost heap turned over to reveal all the mildewed rot in the center.

Christine marched over to the table without hesitation. "What the devil is that?" she exclaimed. "Whyborne, do stop being silly and come over here."

I took out my handkerchief and pressed it to my mouth and nose. The sight of the opened chest, heart and lungs exposed, was ghastly enough. Even worse were the dark, threadlike growths which infiltrated them, seeming to sprout from the spine outward. Odell's brain appeared even more infected.

"Oh God." I turned away and stared resolutely at the wall, trying not to vomit.

"What is it?" Griffin asked, his voice a pale shadow of its usual self. "Some sort of disease?"

Dr. Greene's voice was equally shaky. "I don't know. It has an almost fungal appearance, but I've never heard of an infection presenting like...this. I'd imagine some obscure disease gained in a foreign port, perhaps, but..."

But we were involved, which meant something even more awful might be happening. He left that part unspoken, but the implication was clear.

"I think we've seen enough," Griffin said. I turned back around when the rustle of the sheet assured me the dead man had been covered once again. Christine looked unmoved, which was hardly a surprise, but Griffin's skin had taken on a distinctly greenish hue, and Iskander appeared deeply shaken.

"Is this something I should be concerned about?" Tilton asked, glancing back and forth between us.

The attention of the police was something I'd never desired, even before Griffin came into my life. Now that we lived in the same house and shared the same bed, the possibility of a knock at the door and a sudden arrest always lurked at the back of my mind. Especially as Griffin and Tilton had clashed over cases in the past.

But Tilton had come to us in July, when unnatural forces murdered Griffin's client in jail. Tilton hadn't survived as a police officer in Widdershins without knowing when to look away.

Was I now one of the things he knew to look away from? To pretend he didn't see, just as he would ignore a hooded figure slipping down an alley, or the sound of chanting drifting from a basement?

"We don't know," Griffin answered. "But we are attempting to find out." He paused, then added delicately, "Mr. Delancey dabbled in...matters better left unsaid. Did he have anything of interest in his pockets?"

"A hotel key." Tilton passed it to Griffin. "And a small amount of cash. Nothing else. Odell had even less than that. We wouldn't even have a name for him if you hadn't given it to us."

"Thank you, detective," Griffin said. "Let us know if you learn anything further, if you don't mind."

Tilton's mustache twitched. "I'd prefer not to learn anything further about it, to be honest. But if I do, I'll pass it on to you." He glanced at me as he spoke, and I nodded slightly.

We shuffled out. "Well, that was certainly disturbing," Christine remarked once we reached the viewing room again.

"More than disturbing," I agreed with a shiver. "What the devil *was* that?"

Griffin shook his head. "I don't know. It looked like a physical manifestation of the corruption my shadowsight revealed. Whatever happened to Odell, it wasn't just due to magic or infection, but some unholy union of the two."

"Some creation of the masters?" Iskander suggested. "Like the ketoi and umbrae?"

God, I hoped not. "I'll look at the Wisborg Codex," I said. "Perhaps it will reveal something useful."

"And I'll see what, if anything, Mr. Delancey left in his hotel room," Griffin said, holding up the key. "Perhaps we can find out precisely why the Fideles wished him dead…and why he so urgently wanted to speak to me as well as you."

CHAPTER 5

Griffin

I SLEPT POORLY that night, visions of Odell blending with memories from my childhood. I dreamed Fallow had somehow relocated to the city of the umbrae in Alaska. I ran through the tunnels looking for Ma, while the Mother of Shadows whispered dire warnings into my mind.

Whyborne shook me awake. "It's just a dream," he murmured sleepily into my ear. "You're safe, darling."

I sat up, and the blanket slid to my waist. The chilly fall air raised goosebumps on my arms. Whyborne mumbled a protest and drew the blankets more securely around him. "The Mother of Shadows," I said aloud.

Whyborne blinked. "What about her?"

"If Iskander is right, if this corruption is some creation of the masters, she might know of it." She'd given me the Occultum Lapidem so I could call upon her if needed. I'd used it once already to warn her of the return of the masters. "Or I suppose the ketoi might."

"The umbrae remember things the ketoi have forgotten," Whyborne said, "but I can ask Persephone, if the Mother of Shadows doesn't know." He glanced at the window. Dawn broke outside the window, low gray light filtering around the edges of the curtains. "Is there still time to call upon her before the sun comes up?"

The umbrae were creatures of the night, unable to bear the touch of sunlight. The telepathic link between us worked best in the dark. "No." I sighed. "If only I'd thought of it last night."

"You still have the hotel room to search," Whyborne reminded me. "Come. The alarm will sound in a few minutes anyway, so we might as well dress and have breakfast."

We'd almost finished a breakfast of toast and oatmeal, when a sharp knock sounded on the door. I waved Whyborne back down when he made to answer it, as I was closer.

Detective Tilton loitered on the stoop. Tilton had first reached out for our help in July, and I didn't think he would suddenly decide to arrest us, even if he did have his suspicions as to our relationship. But even the possibility sent a tingle of fear through my extremities, and my mind raced to categorize all the incriminating details sitting out in plain view should he come within. A photograph of the two of us on the couch, in a pose suggesting a certain amount of intimacy; one of Whyborne's scholarly journals left on the dresser of what was ostensibly my bedroom; the spare dressing gown in his wardrobe, far too short for a man of his height. Even the simple domesticity of sharing breakfast and the newspaper before beginning our day might be read as criminal, were Tilton so inclined.

"Detective," I said, loudly enough for Whyborne to hear me in the kitchen. "I must say, I'm surprised to see you this early."

"Believe me, I'd rather be in bed right now," Tilton said. I made no move to let him inside, and he didn't seem to expect an invitation. "But I left orders at the station for anything relating to the case from last night to be brought to my attention immediately. It seems Mr. Odell had a friend who shared a room with him in a boarding house. He grew worried when Odell didn't come home last night, and stopped by the station this morning before going to work."

"Did your men tell him what happened?" I asked.

"No. Said we'd look into it." Tilton rubbed at his jaw. He'd missed a spot while shaving, and he grimaced when he found it. "It seems the roommate worked in the freight sorting yard at the railway depot, along with Mr. Odell. A Mr. Klaus Johansson."

I nodded. "Thank you. I'll speak with him myself."

"Good." Tilton hunched his shoulders beneath his wool overcoat. "As I said last night, I've no interest in learning anything more about this than I have to. This sort of thing is best left to those who know how to take care of it."

As soon as he was gone, Whyborne emerged from the kitchen. No doubt he'd waited for the detective to leave, hoping out of sight equaled out of mind. Or at least made it easier for Tilton to politely ignore our living arrangement. "Tilton has a point," he said.

"What do you mean?"

"I know more about sorcery, and you know more about asking the right questions. Instead of going to the hotel room, why don't you talk to the men at the freight sorting yard?" He held out his hand expectantly. "Christine and I will go to the hotel where Delancey was staying. If there's anything of either archaeological or sorcerous interest in his belongings, we'll find it."

"It's Saturday," I reminded him. "You both have to work a half day."

"Miss Parkhurst and Iskander will lie, should anyone ask our whereabouts. There are enough obscure storerooms that someone could spend all day hunting for us at the museum."

I hesitated, but he was right. Splitting our forces made a certain amount of sense now that we had two different directions in which to investigate. "All right," I said, taking the key from my pocket and passing it to him. "But be careful. Don't handle any strange artifacts unless you're sure they aren't cursed."

He bent and brushed a kiss across my lips. "And you be careful as well."

"I'll be in a busy freight yard in the middle of the day," I reminded him. "I'm certain not even the most determined Fideles agent would dare attack under such circumstances. I'll be perfectly safe."

~ * ~

An hour or two later, I approached the foreman at the freight sorting yard. Although not nearly as large a city as Boston or New York, Widdershins was a port town, and freight of all kinds came and left on the rail lines. The bells of the switch engines rang as they raced back and forth, men shouted as cars coupled and uncoupled, and steam whistles shrieked loudly enough to make my ears ache. The place gave the impression of a very noisy anthill, all frenzied activity, whose pattern presented only confusion to my eye.

I'd dressed in such a fashion as to blend with my surroundings: a suit two years out of date and showing signs of wear around the cuffs, bowler hat, and sturdy boots. My sword cane I reluctantly left at home, but I brought my revolver just in case.

I also carried a small stack of bills to keep both foreman and workers well-disposed to me. "Mr. Johansson?" the foreman mused, and I discreetly slipped him another folded bill. "Ah, yes. I believe he's unloading lumber at the moment. I'll send him your way."

I dallied at the edge of the yard, watching men swarm over boxcars, shifting freight from rail to wagon or to ship. Soon enough, I was joined by a tall, lanky man with a ready smile and hair in need of a trim. "Mr. Johansson?"

"Ja," he said, shaking my hand. "You want to speak to me? Is this about Cotton?"

"It is," I agreed. "Can you tell me anything that might help us find him?"

Perhaps he assumed me a detective with the police. Or perhaps he didn't care about my motive, so long as someone was looking for his friend. "What do you need to know?"

"Anything that might seem of interest," I said with studied casualness. "His habits. His background. Any unusual changes in his behavior. How long have you known him?"

"Not long." Johansson took out his handkerchief and absently wiped sweat and grime from his brow. "Under two months, perhaps? We share a little room not far from here. As for his habits, there's not much to tell. We wake up, come to work, get dinner and a beer or two after, and go home again." He shrugged.

I itched to ask more direct questions, but I didn't want Johansson to realize I'd once known Mr. Odell. "No sweetheart, then?"

"Nein, nein." Johansson shook his head. "The man doesn't even play cards. That's why I went straight to the police when he didn't come home last night. I expected them to laugh me off, say he must be drunk somewhere, that I would have to fight to get anyone to take this seriously."

"We're taking this quite seriously, I assure you." I considered a moment, before asking the question I'd wanted to from the start. "Do you know anything about his background? Where he came from, what brought him to Widdershins, anything like that?"

"A little." Johansson took out a battered cigarette case and offered me one. When I declined, he lit one for himself. "He came from somewhere to the west. Kansas, I think. He was a farmer. Influenza carried off his entire family in '94."

I tried and failed to recall how many children Odell had. Two daughters and three sons? Or was it four?

Had the tragedy broken his mind in some fashion? Driven him into the arms of the Fideles? "God rest their souls."

"Ja." Johansson nodded sadly. "He tried to go on, but he was not a young man, and his heart was broken. He lost everything and was taken in by the—how do you say it? The poor farm?"

If Odell hadn't tried to kill me less than twenty-four hours ago, I would have felt sorry for the man. To have fallen from a respected position in the community, surrounded by family and friends, to a pauper surviving only on the charity of the county, must have been a terrible blow. "Then how did he come to Widdershins?" I asked.

Johansson tossed down the butt of his cigarette and ground it out with his boot. "He didn't say, other than fate had intervened. If you really want to know, talk to our other roommate."

I frowned. "Other roommate?"

"Monroe Evers. He came from Kansas with Cotton." Johansson nodded in the direction he'd come from. "He's working with me right over there."

My heart kicked against my ribs. Monroe Evers.

We'd blackened each other's eyes as boys. He'd been a year older than me, the sort of child who pulled wings off of flies. Anything smaller than him had been a target—and he'd been large for his age.

My hands curled into fists, pulse rushing faster. Delancey had asked to talk to me, Odell attempted to kill me, and now here was another person from Fallow.

Perhaps I'd been too quick to assure Whyborne of my safety.

"Can you take me to him?" I asked.

Johansson nodded and loped off. I followed him through the freight yard, pausing to let the switch engines whisk past and dodging around lines of cars waiting to be unloaded. The clang of bells and couplers, the hiss of air brakes, the shouts of men, dinned against my ears. As Johansson said, Odell was no longer a young man. After a lifetime of farming, of being his own master, it must have seemed strange and terrible to work here, for a wage that would barely afford him food and a place to stay. Then again, perhaps it had been a welcome escape from the memories of his dead family, of the happy times they'd once spent in the fields and barns.

Or perhaps Odell simply felt he had nothing left to live for. Was that how the Fideles had recruited him to kill Delancey?

Johansson led the way to a group of flatcars, some still piled high with lumber. "Monroe!" he yelled to one of the men who'd just unfastened a load. "There's a man here who wants to talk to you about Cotton!"

Monroe Evers turned to us. In his hands, he held the now-loose chain that had secured the lumber, one end capped with a large hook. The midmorning sun cast shade over his features from the brim of his hat, but my shadowsight perceived the corruption crawling over his skin.

~ * ~

For a moment, we only stared at one another. Then his expression shifted from one of curiosity—to pure fury.

I barely had time to duck as the hook whistled over my head. Johansson cried out, as did the men of the work crew, but Evers didn't seem to even hear them. Instead, he leapt down from his perch, swinging the chain so the hook sliced viciously through the air.

"You'll pay for what you did," he growled.

I had no way to defend myself from the chain, save for my revolver—and there were too many other men crowded around to risk hitting one of them. I ducked as he lashed at me again, then broke into a run.

Evers lumbered after me. I bolted across one set of tracks, then another, before ducking between two rows of boxcars. The tracks were close together, forcing me to turn almost sideways to fit through. Even as I did so, the line of boxcars on my right began to move. I pressed myself more tightly to the other cars; if I wasn't careful of my feet, I'd lose them. Or possibly more.

As soon as the line of boxcars cleared my position, I caught the glint of sunlight on the chain. Evers had been waiting.

I dropped into a crouch, and the hook slammed against the side of the car behind me—and caught on the cut lever. Seizing my opportunity, I lunged to my feet, burying the top of my head in Evers's stomach. He let out a startled "oof," and staggered back, but didn't go down.

No matter. I pulled out my revolver and held it to his temple. "Mr. Evers—"

No shadow of fear passed over his face. As if uncaring for his life, he pivoted on his heel and slammed his fist into my side.

The unexpected blow sent me tumbling onto the next set of tracks. A bell clanged madly, and I looked up, only to see the front of a switch engine bearing down on me.

I hurled myself forward, praying the next set of tracks would be clear. Even as I did so, Evers lunged after me, as insensible to the danger of the engine as he had been of the gun.

There came a horrible, wet crunch. The engineer let out a cry of horror, and air brakes hissed. Men shouted and came running from every direction.

"Mein Gott!" Johansson crouched beside me, his fair face even paler with fear. "Are you hurt?"

I shook my head and allowed him to help me to my feet. My trousers were ripped and my palms abraded, but otherwise I'd escaped without harm.

The same couldn't be said for Evers.

I turned away from the sight of tracks smeared red with blood. Why had he acted with such indifference to his own safety? Surely he wouldn't have survived his job here for more than a few days if that was his normal behavior.

Instead, it was as if he'd been so focused on hurting me nothing else mattered. Not even his own life.

"Why did he do that?" Johansson asked, staring past me in horror at the ruin of what had been a human being. "Why did he attack you?"

"I don't know," I said. But I was going to have to find out.

CHAPTER 6

Whyborne

"WAIT." **I PUT** a hand on Christine's elbow as we entered the Widdershins Arms Hotel. As hotels went, it was quite respectable, if not luxurious. Men and women sat in the lobby, reading the paper or chatting. Fortunately, none of them looked our way.

"What is it, Whyb—that is, I mean, Mr. Weatherby? My husband?" Christine asked loudly. Now *everyone* was looking at us.

I'd taken a bit of inspiration from Griffin's aptitude for blending into the background whenever he carried out an investigation. I'd become all too recognizable in town as of late; people might notice and wonder what I was about, letting myself into a hotel room when I had a perfectly serviceable house nearby. So I'd looted through Griffin's small collection of eyeglasses, false noses, and wigs, before settling on a false mustache applied with spirit gum. Between the mustache and the bowler hat I'd borrowed, I was certain no one would easily recognize me.

Christine wore a very large feathered hat, to which she'd attached several additional ostrich plumes, in the hopes it would both hide and distract from her face. If anyone asked, we would claim to be the Weatherbys, newlyweds vacationing in Widdershins.

"Keep your voice down, dear," I said, casting a smile at a couple staring at us. Lowering my voice, I added, "Should we ask for Delancey's mail at the desk?"

"On our way out," she decided. "That way, if the clerk remembers Delancey and grows suspicious, we won't get thrown out before we even reach the room."

"Good idea," I whispered back. A glance showed me the couple were still staring. "Quick—take my arm."

"Whatever for?"

"We're supposed to be newlyweds."

Muttering something under her breath, she seized my arm in a vise-like grip. "Come along, Whyb—husband," she said, dragging me toward the stairs. Would the watching couple assume an excess of marital enthusiasm on her part? It would no doubt help our disguise if they did, but the very thought made me feel a bit faint.

Thankfully, no one questioned our right to be in the hotel. We passed one or two maids, but otherwise the hallways seemed deserted. According to the number on the key, Delancey's room was on the top floor at one corner, as though he wished to be surrounded by as few people as possible.

A maid was busy changing the linens in the next room. She glanced our way, then frowned. "I haven't done your room, sir, ma'am," she said, staring rather curiously at my face. "I can get it right quick, if you want, or—"

"Come back later," Christine said, unlocking the room. She still hadn't let go of my arm.

"Er, yes," I said to the maid. "We're newlyweds, you see, and—"

"Stop dawdling and get inside, man!"

I glimpsed the maid doubled over in silent laughter before Christine forcefully shut the door. "Christine!" I hissed at her. My face flamed, and I briefly considered crawling beneath the bed and expiring from sheer embarrassment.

"Oh, quit complaining. She won't be back for hours," Christine said. "Now let's have a look around."

The room contained a clothespress, bed, washstand, and desk. "Check the desk," I told Christine, and bent to peer beneath the bed. "Oh, look!"

She turned from the desk. "You found something?"

"A penny." I held it up.

She rolled her eyes. "If it isn't an enchanted penny, I suggest you keep looking."

I tucked the penny in my pocket and opened the clothespress. A single suit hung inside, accompanied by two shirts and a tie. A small trunk had also been shoved in the back.

I pulled the trunk out and placed it on the bed. Fortunately, the key was still in the lock, so I opened it easily.

I'd hoped for some obvious clue—a book of spells like the *Arcanorum*, or a diary detailing everything which had brought Delancey to Widdershins. Instead, I found a supply of cheap cuffs and collars, a loofah bath brush, and a package of pills promising to "cure all desire for tobacco." At the very bottom were a handful of photographs.

I lifted them out. The top one showed a group of men, including Delancey, standing around some sort of tall machinery. Around them stretched an expanse of barren land, the soil cracked and broken.

"What do you make of this?" I asked Christine, holding out the photo.

She glanced at it. "It looks to be some sort of drilling apparatus."

Several other photos showed the same men and machinery, in various states of operation and setup. Though the landscape immediately around them remained bare earth, a house or barn showed in the distance of some of the photographs, making me think they'd drilled in multiple locations. I flipped over the photos, and found writing on the back of one.

"Fideles located the transferal sphere at a depth of 203 feet," I read aloud. "The Fideles...but he's posing with them."

"Perhaps he infiltrated the cult. Or was working with them and changed his mind." Christine shrugged. "I'm more interested in this transferal sphere. Do you think that refers to the artifact Delancey had in his valise?"

"Probably. Though that doesn't tell us what it was transferring."

Christine straightened. "Whyborne, look at this."

I joined her at the desk. She handed me a punched train ticket, which Delancey must have absent-mindedly tossed in the drawer when he reached the hotel. The ticket bore the familiar Whyborne Railroad crest, and the conductor's stamp matched the date of the postmark on Delancey's letter from Topeka.

"Look at the city of origin," Christine said. "He took the train to Topeka…from Fallow."

Delancey had come from Fallow, just as Odell had earlier. "The photographs," I said, snatching one up. "What did Griffin say about a barren spot, which gave the place its name? Could that be why the land looks so arid around the drilling apparatus?"

A sharp knock sounded on the door.

~ * ~

Christine and I exchanged a look of alarm. Surely the maid wouldn't have returned so soon, unless she discovered we weren't the room's legitimate occupants.

"Newlyweds," Christine muttered. "Right."

Before I could ask what she was on about, she clambered onto the bed and began to jump enthusiastically on it. "Oh!" she shouted above the squeaking frame. "Yes! There! There!"

"Christine?" Iskander called through the closed door. "Is that you?"

Oh God. Visions of Iskander hurling me from the window flashed through my mind.

"Oh," Christine said, climbing down from the bed and throwing open the door. "Hello, Kander. We weren't expecting you."

"So I see," Iskander said dryly. Thank heavens he didn't look homicidal. "What on earth is on your head?"

"Never mind that," Griffin said, stepping in behind him. "What the devil is attached to your face, Whyborne?"

"It's a disguise," I said, a bit smug that I'd thought to use it.

His lips started to twitch. "The purpose of a disguise is to divert attention, not make everyone wonder why you're going about town with a dead caterpillar on your lip."

I scowled at him and tore the false mustache off. My angry gesture was undermined by the fact it stung more than I'd expected.

"We decided to pose as newlyweds," Christine explained, nodding so that Iskander had to duck to avoid one of the plumes sprouting from her hat.

"It wasn't a terrible idea, in theory," he said neutrally. Unfortunately, the spastic twitches of the corners of his mouth betrayed him.

"Indeed." Griffin grinned at me. "The two of you could teach the Pinkertons some tricks."

"Oh, do be quiet," I muttered, sinking down to the edge of the bed. The tiny room was horribly crowded with the four of us plus Christine's giant hat. "What are you two doing here?"

"After I finished up at the train yard, I came to see you at the museum. Iskander said you'd left for the hotel. We decided to lend our assistance."

Christine looked annoyed. "I think Whyborne and I are quite capable of searching a room by ourselves."

"Unless someone was watching for Delancey's return and saw you come in here," Griffin replied, all mirth gone from his face now.

Something must have gone wrong, to cause him additional concern. "What happened?"

"I was attacked," Griffin said. "By another corrupted man, whom I knew from Fallow."

I stood back up and reached for him. "Are you all right?"

"Just a few bruises." Griffin's expression was somber. "As for him, he ended up beneath the wheels of a switch engine."

"Oh my." I sat down again. "We found punched train tickets. It seems as though Delancey was in Fallow as well. And we found this." I handed him the stack of photos. "Judging by the writing on the back of the photo, the artifact was brought up by one of the drilling attempts…"

I trailed off. In the afternoon light streaming through the window, Griffin's face had gone stark white. "Oh God," he whispered.

"It's the fallow spot, isn't it?" I asked uncertainly.

"Yes, but…" He held out the photo with the writing on the back. "Can you see the barn in the distance. And beyond it a house?"

"Yes?"

"It's the house I was raised in. Ma's house." Griffin swallowed. "If the Fideles are there…she's in terrible danger."

CHAPTER 7

Griffin

"WE HAVE TO go to Fallow. At once," I said as I unlocked the door to our house. My mind raced feverishly, ticking through a list of things that needed to be done.

"Griffin," Whyborne said as he followed me inside. Iskander and Christine trailed after him.

"Train schedules first," I said. "Then we have to decide what to pack."

"Griffin," Whyborne repeated.

"I'm sure Mrs. Yates will look after Saul—we'll have to stop in on our way to the station in the morning—"

"Griffin!"

I'd started up the stairs, and so for once found myself looking down on him. The light found the tiny lines creasing the corners of his eyes, the familiar curve of his lips.

"Calm down," he said. "We need to consider this rationally and plan our next move."

Something tightened in my chest, like a strand of barbed wire looped around my heart. "My mother is in danger."

Christine stepped up behind him. "We know that, but we can't help her if we don't even know what the danger is."

"Of course you take his side!"

"I say!" exclaimed Iskander. I ignored his protest and stormed up the rest of the stairs into the study. They didn't understand. They *couldn't* understand.

Whyborne grabbed me by the shoulder before I reached the door to my room. "Christine isn't taking my side, blast it! There isn't a side to take, except the one we're all on."

"Then let go of me and pack your bags!"

His hold tightened. "Calm down. Take a breath. We have to think this through, not go haring off half-cocked."

I wrenched free. "When has that ever stopped us before?"

Whyborne sighed. "As you wish." He turned to Christine. "Christine, as I can't ask you to throw away your career by leaving without so much as securing permission from the director, you and Iskander must remain here. No, don't protest—I'll need you to take in Saul. And someone will have to tell Persephone that she'll need to face the return of the masters alone, as I'll be dead in a ditch in Kansas."

I gritted my teeth. "Damn it, Whyborne. I'll go by myself."

"Don't be absurd." Anger flashed in his dark eyes as he turned back to me. "You are my husband, and I will not abandon you."

"Whyborne..." The barbed wire dug in deeper. "You don't understand. In the freight yard, Mr. Evers was fine—normal—until he saw me."

"He was corrupted," Whyborne interrupted. "That isn't normal."

"Normal in behavior, then." I swallowed. "He said the same thing as Odell. *'You'll pay for what you did.'* Then he attacked me. He behaved as though killing me was more important than preserving his own life." I spread my hands helplessly. "Even Delancey asked to see me when he wrote to you. Whatever is going on in Fallow, it's connected to me in some way. If something happens to Ma and it's my fault..."

"But you haven't even been back to Fallow in years," Christine protested. "How on earth could this have anything to do with you?"

Iskander sat on the couch, brow furrowed. "And there's no reason these fellows might have a grudge against you?"

"Enough of a grudge for Evers to ignore a gun at his head? To fling himself in front of a switch engine while attempting to get at me?"

I sank down on the couch. "And Odell—he knew there were armed security guards right there at the museum. He'd spoken to them on his way in. Instead of surrendering or fleeing, he chose to attack me, even though he surely realized it would provoke them to fire."

"It does seem you'd remember doing something awful enough to instigate such behavior," Christine observed.

"We all saw the infection in Odell's brain," Whyborne said. "I'd be greatly surprised if either man was in his right mind. Perhaps their rage was due to that, rather than anything Griffin actually did?"

"You could be right," I agreed. "And if they were Fideles—if they were recruited when the cult came to Fallow to drill—they may simply have recognized me as one of the people who prevented the Fideles from a full victory last July. Combined with the infection's effect on their brains…"

"Right now, all we have is speculation." Whyborne perched beside me, on the arm of the couch. "Griffin, listen to us, please. Allow Christine to take the sphere to the director—I'm certain he'll give her permission to investigate where it was found. I'll look through the Wisborg Codex and the Pnakotic Manuscripts, in hopes I might discover some clue as to how to combat the corruption you described. For now, as soon as night falls, speak to the Mother of Shadows. I'll go to Persephone. One of them might know something that will help us."

"Quite," Iskander said. "And even if we learn nothing, we won't leave your mother in danger, Griffin. We'll accompany you to Fallow."

They were right, of course. Despite my fear for Ma, I couldn't help but feel a rush of relief and gratitude. In truth, I had no desire to return to Fallow alone…and not only because of the dangers posed by the Fideles. Walking its streets again, seeing the faces of those I had known as a child, who remembered why I'd abruptly left town, would likely not be easy. "Thank you, Iskander. That means a great deal."

~ * ~

I carefully took the Occultum Lapidem from the locked cabinet in my office and placed it on my desk. The irregularly-cut gem sat on a brass stand, and the light of the lone candle at my elbow seemed swallowed by its purple-black depths. Veins of red pulsed deep within, as though it were in some way alive.

A strange object to take comfort in, and yet I did. The Mother of Shadows had given it to me so that we might communicate, but also, I thought, so I wouldn't feel alone. I had never used it to speak with her save when dictated by necessity…but I could have whenever I chose, and that mattered.

I'd convinced Whyborne it was safe to leave me unguarded while he went to the beach and spoke with Persephone. The memory of his worried expression cut deep, though. I'd wanted to lighten his burdens. Instead, I'd added to them.

I blew out the candle, plunging the room into darkness. It was well after midnight; according to Whyborne's rough calculations, the sun should have set in the far latitude where the city of shadows lay hidden beneath the glacier.

The gem's facets were smooth beneath my hands. As soon as I touched it, I heard a soft whispering, as if a gathering of people stood in the kitchen or above in the study, all of them murmuring together.

The umbrae weren't like humans, or even the ketoi. Some of them were hatched as soldiers, protecting their colony and hunting food outside. The workers took care of the young, kept the nest clean, and farmed the fungal growths that served as the mainstay of their food. All of them communicated instantly with one another via a sort of telepathy. The Mother of Shadows ruled over the nest; a queen whose intelligence was informed instantly by whatever a worker or solider discovered. They were her children; she guided them, cared for them, and ensured the survival of the nest for the next queen to take over.

We were as unlike as it was possible for two beings to be. And yet, in the grief and love we bore for our families, we'd discovered common ground.

I took a deep breath to clear my mind. Then I concentrated on my last glimpse of the Mother of Shadows, her vast, segmented body disappearing into the darkness of the great hall where she lived. On the words we'd spoken with nothing more than thought. Mainly, I focused on a single emotion, the one which had connected us in the first place.

My love for Ma, and my longing to be reconciled with her someday.

"My child. You have need of me?"

I felt as though some tight band inside loosened slightly. Not entirely, but a notch, just enough so I could breathe again. "Yes," I said aloud. "There is something…we think it might be a creation of the masters."

I offered up images in place of words, as far more efficient. And felt her recoil, with the same disgust I had experienced.

"I do not know this corruption," she said at last. *"But that means little. The masters created many tools."* A flash of hatred from her, directed at the masters, the creators and enslavers of the umbrae. *"You must be cautious."*

A headache began to form behind my eyes. Telepathic speech came naturally to the umbrae, but my human brain was another matter. "I will."

"You fear for your mother."

I hadn't said as much, but she'd plucked it from my mind anyway. It was a relief, in a way, not to have to put so much into words. "Of course I do. She doesn't know about any of…this."

"She believes an illusion, that the world has been built for and ordered by humans. That what she considers reality is solid, not a thin skin stretched tight over the truth of the universe."

I tasted blood in the back of my throat as my headache grew fiercer. "I don't want her to learn differently. I want her to sleep peacefully, not wake screaming in the dark. I don't want her to be touched by the pain and the fear, and the constant striving, one evil vanquished just so another can take its place."

Grief and understanding. But: *"She is not a child."*

"No," I agreed heavily. "But once you know the truth about things…you can't un-know it." I shook my head. "Forgive me. I just want to protect her."

"And what of you?" A phantom caress brushed my face. *"You speak to me of the masters, of your human mother. But not of yourself."*

What could I tell her that she couldn't already guess? I feared we'd fail, the masters would return, and I'd see everyone I loved die screaming. Darkness lay behind my husband's eyes; he no longer laughed, and a distance seemed to be forming between us despite my best efforts to bridge it. Surely she'd already seen it all in my thoughts.

"Do not lose yourself to fear, child." The pain in my head spiked, and the Mother of Shadows began to withdraw, our thoughts slowly spiraling apart. *"Your strength has always been to see with the eyes of your heart. Do not let fear blind you, else you will surely lose that which you love most."*

CHAPTER 8

Whyborne

THE WAVES CRASHED on the sand, rolling nearly to my feet as I paced back and forth along the strand. The full moon hung overhead, its light sparkling on the foam. Persephone sat on a tide-worn rock, her tentacle hair curling about her shoulders.

"I know nothing of this corruption you describe," she said when I finished. Her tendril hair writhed in distress. "Or why they should wish to kill your husband."

It had been a slim hope anyway. "Then I must leave. You'll have to stand guard over the land and the sea while I'm gone."

"The ketoi have eyes on the land," she reminded me. "Or have you forgotten? I will send word to those of our blood who live above the waves."

I stopped my pacing. "No. Widdershins is our responsibility. We shouldn't put any more people in harm's way than necessary."

The moonlight gleamed from her golden jewelry. It would have looked absurd on a human woman, at least in modern times, but it fit her fierce appearance in a way something more delicate wouldn't have. "They wish to aid us, brother."

I shook my head and went back to pacing. "This is our fight. Yours and mine."

"Father will help. And the librarians. As they did before."

The scars pulled tight over my knuckles as I clenched my fists. Why didn't she understand? "Aren't you listening?" I demanded, rounding on her. "I'm not going to let people die just because the damnable maelstrom *collected* them!" I shook my head. "You didn't experience what I did. You and I are just—just parts of this *thing* that the masters created so they could pass back and forth between our world and the Outside. The maelstrom isn't human, or ketoi; it's not even a person. It calls people here, to this place, because it doesn't want to be used by the masters. So it hypocritically uses others."

I kicked angrily at a shell, but succeeded only in knocking sand into my shoe. "It can't undo what's already been done, but I won't let anyone else suffer on its behalf. It created you and me, so we're responsible. No one else."

She hissed at me, showing teeth. "You sound like a land-dweller, brother. Stupid."

I glared at her "I beg your pardon!"

"Ketoi work together." She rose to her feet and gestured to the waves. "We know we cannot survive alone, so we fight, or harvest algae, or hunt according to our skills." Her teeth showed again in an angry grimace. "But just as there are those who still wish for war against the humans, there are some who desire the return of the masters. They believe the masters will give ketoi rule of the sea and drown the ships of the land dwellers. If I tried to face them alone, I would die." Her eyes, so like my own, fixed on my face. "You cannot do this alone either, brother."

She didn't understand. "I'm part of something that has—has warped and perverted the lives of those I love most." I shook my head. "Perhaps it's different for the ketoi. Do as you wish beneath the waves, but the land is my responsibility. And I won't debate this any further with you."

I turned and walked away, a mixture of anger and resentment seething in my gut. As I started up the path toward the main road, however, she called out after me. "Ask your husband what he wishes. Widdershins always knows its own."

"I wish I'd never heard those words," I shot back.

I fumed all the way home. Of course Persephone thought nothing of ordering people around. She was a chieftess among the ketoi, after all. She probably got the disposition from Father; God knew one of us had to inherit something from him.

I let myself into the darkened house—then paused before turning on the lights. Griffin's voice drifted from the parlor. Apparently he'd been successful in reaching the Mother of Shadows.

"I don't want her to learn differently," Griffin said plaintively. "I want her to sleep peacefully, not wake screaming in the dark. I don't want her to be touched by the pain and the fear, and the constant striving, one evil vanquished just so another can take its place."

I didn't hear the Mother of Shadows's answer. But then, I didn't need to, did I?

Griffin regretted the pain and the fear, the constant striving that the maelstrom had inflicted on him. He wanted to keep Nella from experiencing such a thing—and how could I possibly blame him?

He sighed heavily, in response to some comment from the Mother of Shadows. "No. But once you know the truth about things...you can't un-know it."

No. No you couldn't.

I could never unlearn that the maelstrom had brought him here. Or that I was a part of the maelstrom.

Or that he regretted the course his life had taken, and wished to spare anyone else from it.

There came the sound of him moving about in the darkened room. I switched on the hall light. A moment later, he stepped into the hall, squinting against the brightness. "Ival. What did Persephone say?"

"She didn't know anything."

Another sigh from him. "Neither did the Mother of Shadows. I'd hoped...but there's nothing to be done."

"No." I slipped my arms around him, drawing him close. "Even so, we'll go to Fallow and protect your mother, Griffin. I swear it."

And perhaps...perhaps they would even reconcile. If he had her back, surely he wouldn't need me as much. Surely he'd be content to stay in Fallow, away from darkness and death.

At least for a while; if the masters returned, Fallow would be as threatened as anywhere else. He could stay and protect Nella, his cousins, whoever else needed him.

He'd argue, if I suggested he stay. Say he wouldn't leave me to face the masters alone.

So I'd have to tell him the truth. About me. About what I'd done to him.

Griffin tipped his head back, and I kissed him softly. Memorizing the taste of his lips, the feel of him in my arms. I couldn't tell him just yet, not until we saw to whatever threatened Fallow now.

We had a little time left, at least.

CHAPTER 9

Griffin

I STARED OUT the window of the train car, the earth a flat expanse of green and dusty brown, gilded in the lowering light of the sun. A lone tree jutted up just ahead, marking the bank of Dogleg Creek. The creek marked the official boundary of Fallow. Legend had it early settlers had hung outlaws from the tree, as it was the only one on the nearby plains tall enough for such rough justice.

The tree had died at some point in my absence. Only a thick trunk still remained, its once-lush branches fallen away.

I couldn't help but recall my previous glimpses of the tree. Today, I travelled in luxury—Niles had provided his private car, complete with plush seats, a dining table draped in white cloth, a liquor cabinet, and comfortable sleeper beds. Whyborne dozed in the seat beside me, long legs stretched out into the wide aisle. Iskander read a book, and Christine scowled at some notes she'd been scribbling.

This return was incalculably different from my first arrival. Then, I'd been utterly alone in the world, my parents and sister dead, my older brothers adopted off the orphan train at previous stops along the route. All I had left of them was Jack's coat wrapped around my shoulders, its sleeves so long they covered my hands. I had nothing but the coat and my name when I stepped onto the depot platform.

The adults had seemed so big, so strange and frightening. I didn't know whether to hope one of them would choose me, or to fear it. If no one wanted me, what would happen? Would I be returned to the Children's Aid Society in New York? Or simply be put off the train at the last stop and told to fend for myself?

Then one of the men dropped into a crouch in front of me. Sun and weather had tanned his skin, and his bristling beard frightened me at first. But the smile he offered was kind. "What's your name, son?"

I'd gone home with him that day. Back to the farmhouse meant to provide shelter for the half a dozen children fate had ultimately failed to grant. His wife proved to be just as kindly, greeting me with a smile and a slice of fresh-baked apple pie.

I'd never tasted anything half so good.

They told me to call them Ma and Pa, and put me to bed amidst warm blankets, beneath a sound roof. I'd never slept alone before, and as I watched the shadows of a tree sway across the wall opposite the wide window, I felt a new touch of fear. Not of the dark, or anything in it. Rather, that this would all be taken away. That my new parents would change their minds and put me back on the next orphan train.

That I'd be truly alone again.

I swore then I'd do anything to please them. I'd be the son they wanted, and never give them an instant of regret for choosing me instead of some other lad.

I managed to keep that oath for years. But in the end, I failed them after all. And just as I'd feared, they brought me to the depot and put me on a train—although this one had been bound for Chicago, and I'd been a young man, not a child, by then.

The brightness of an arcane line flashed past, and I blinked. Whyborne stirred slightly and mumbled something in his sleep. We'd crossed over a few such lines since leaving Widdershins, naturally, but I hadn't expected one so close to Fallow.

"How is the paper coming?" I asked Christine, hoping for a distraction.

"Bah!" She sat back in her seat, her scowl deepening. "I can't help but wonder if it would be safe to return to the fane of Nyarlathotep. The daemon—the umbra, that is—is gone, after all. I might have lost the firman for the tomb site, but perhaps I could persuade them to let me dig far out in the desert." A wicked smile curved her lips. "They'd assume there would be nothing to find, after all."

Iskander arched a brow. "Considering you were attacked by mummies and faceless statues, I doubt that the absence of the daemon renders the site much safer."

"I suppose." She looked at Whyborne speculatively. He'd started to drool on his shoulder in his sleep. "But Whyborne is much better at pulling magic from arcane lines now. Maybe…"

"We should probably wait until after we're certain the masters aren't about to return and destroy the world," I said.

"I suppose." She didn't look at all happy about the delay.

The train began to slow. Whyborne blinked awake as the porter moved to gather our things. "Are we there?"

I peered out the window and glimpsed the cluster of buildings forming the town proper. I wasn't certain if there were more than the last time I'd left, after my rescue from the asylum. "Yes."

"Thank heavens," Christine said, stretching in her seat. "I hope the hotel has decent whiskey."

I forced a grin onto my face, despite my melancholy thoughts. "I'm afraid the temperance movement reached Kansas before you, Christine. You'd best avail yourself of Niles's private stock before we leave the train."

A look of horror crossed her face. "Good gad, man, you might have warned us! I'd have packed a few bottles in my trunk."

The porter returned with a bottle of rather expensive whiskey from the cabinet. "Perhaps ma'am would care to take this with her?"

"You've saved my life." She took it and stashed it in her valise.

I was first onto the platform, while everyone else gathered their coats and hats. I took a deep breath, feeling as if some invisible hand reached into my chest and squeezed my heart tight. Beneath the smell of burning coal from the train, I recognized the scents of my childhood: dust and dry grass, livestock and fresh cut corn. Enormous grain elevators towered nearby, their sides painted orange by the light of the setting sun. Soon the corn harvest would be finished, and the grain loaded into train cars and shipped to the hungry cities of the east.

Pa had taken pride in that. He wasn't just feeding his own family —our yield nourished families we'd never meet.

And if those families included men like myself, like Whyborne…

would he have been so proud then? Or would he have preferred to keep the corn from their mouths?

"Griffin?" Whyborne said softly from just behind me.

I shook myself back to the present. "Just remembering," I said, as lightly as I could. "Is everyone ready? Then let's go into Fallow."

~ * ~

"Well," said Iskander. "This is a problem."

We stood in the dusty street in front of the hotel. The very closed hotel, its windows shuttered and its door boarded.

A great many of Fallow's buildings were abandoned. The general store remained open, as did the post office, pharmacy, and barber shop. But in between the businesses still clinging to life, weathered signs and empty displays showed the demise of a book shop, jewelry store, photographer, and more. Including, of course, the hotel. Someone had plastered notices on the door and windows: a livestock sale, an upcoming community dance, a sun-faded political advertisement.

Only a few people were about in the streets, and they stared at us curiously. We must indeed present an odd picture, all of us dressed like city folk, our baggage sitting in the road around us. "I'm sorry," I said. "I assumed…"

"Not your fault," Iskander said. "We didn't have time to send ahead and do a proper job of securing the necessities."

Christine heaved a sigh. "Back to the private car, then. At least it will give us a place to sleep."

A wagon rumbling down the street slowed as it approached us. "Griffin? Griffin Flaherty?"

I turned, bracing myself to be attacked again, as I had been in Widdershins.

It took a moment to recognize the red haired man driving the wagon. Sun and wind had burned his fair skin and added lines to his eyes, but his smile took me back to days spent sitting on a rough bench in the little schoolhouse. "Lawrence Reynolds?"

Lawrence let out a happy laugh and climbed down. I reached out to shake his hand—and found myself hauled into a rough embrace.

I hugged him back; he smelled of sweat and cows. I'd last seen him a few days before I was caught with Benjamin, but we'd been friends throughout our childhoods. I'd never thought he might miss me.

"Well, look at you," he said, stepping back, his hand still resting on my shoulder. "All dressed up fancy, like you never heard of work."

I laughed wryly. "True enough. I'm a detective in my ordinary line."

"So no work at all." But he grinned as he said it. "I never expected to lay eyes on you again, that's for sure. So what brings you back here?"

I introduced my companions. Our story was an artifact from Fallow had been donated to the museum, and that we were here to see if any more might be found. "We meant to stay in the hotel, but…" I finished.

"It closed down going on three months ago," Lawrence said with a shake of his head. "What with the drought and all, there ain't much cause for people to come to this part of Kansas, I reckon." He hesitated for a moment, glancing at us and our baggage. I half-expected him to ask why we weren't staying with Ma, but he instead he said, "Well, shoot. Why don't you folks come stay with me and the family? Our house ain't no fancy hotel, and a couple of you fellows might have to sleep in the hayloft, but it's a place to lay your heads."

"The hayloft?" Whyborne asked with some trepidation.

"We shouldn't wish to inconvenience you," Iskander said.

"Ain't no inconvenience." Lawrence grinned. "Just wait till the missus finds out we've got the lady archaeologist and a railroad tycoon staying with us. Every other woman in Fallow will be dying of jealousy."

I shook Lawrence's hand gratefully. "Of course we'll help out with whatever chores we can. I still remember how to milk a cow."

Whyborne looked horrified. "Milk a cow?"

I clapped him on the arm. "I'm sure there's manure to shovel, too."

"That there is," Lawrence agreed. Then he seemed to hesitate, his gaze going to Iskander, then back to me uncertainly. "Listen, one thing I ought to mention. My wife, Annie—she and her folks were exodusters, came here in '79."

"She's black," I translated, since my companions only looked blankly at him.

"Our marriage ain't illegal here in Kansas," Lawrence said defensively, "but if you've an objection, you might want to stay somewhere else."

By his tone, it was clear there were those in Fallow who very much objected. "Not at all," Iskander said.

Lawrence grinned in relief. "I didn't figure you would, seeing as you ain't white yourself, but folks can be funny about these kinds of things. Well, then let's get your baggage in the wagon." He glanced at the setting sun. "We'd best get home before sundown, else Annie will start worrying."

~ * ~

The Reynolds farm was to the west of town: a snug, single-story house accompanied by a barn and chicken coop. A great cloud of dust billowed out behind the wagon as we approached, the dry earth disturbed by the slightest movement and encompassing us all in the choking cloud of fine grit.

Lawrence's wife awaited us on the porch, a lantern in her hand. "I've brought some folks in need of hospitality, Annie," he said.

Annie was a tall woman, with burnt umber skin and a penetrating stare. She wore a cheerful red headscarf, and a flour-dusted apron covered her calico dress. "I'm sorry for the unexpectedness of our visit, Mrs. Reynolds," I said after Lawrence made introductions.

"It's no trouble," she said with a smile. That might not be strictly true—in fact, it probably wasn't—but putting up travelers for a night or two without complaint was an old Kansas tradition, lingering from a time when isolated sod houses had been the only shelter for a hundred miles. "Put down your things and wash up, and I'll have the boys lay some extra places at the table."

The farmhouse consisted of three rooms—a kitchen, a bedroom belonging to Lawrence and Annie, and the large front room that served all other functions. Three boys, long-legged and lean as colts, hastened to lay out more places at the table and bring in water for washing, under their father's doting eye. Before long, we sat down to a meal of boiled ham, chow-chow, pickled beans, and bread slathered with butter.

"So, Griffin, what have you been doing with yourself?" Lawrence asked. "You said you were a detective?"

"I used to work with the Pinkertons," I replied. "But I've come back to help Dr. Putnam-Barnett find her way around the community."

"Did you really dig up that old pharaoh?" asked Simon, the eldest of the Reynolds children. He had his father's eyes and his mother's mouth. "We read about it in school last year."

"I did," Christine said. "Although of course Iskander helped."

"A bit," Iskander said with a wink.

Ordinarily, I would have spent the meal entertaining the gathering with stories of various exploits from my days in the Pinkertons. Chasing bank robbers and foiling train heists was always good for conversation, I'd found. Exciting, but without revealing anything personal about myself.

But none of my tales could hope to compete with Christine's stories of excavating in Egypt. Children and adults both sat enrapt at her anecdotes of charging hippos, blistering heat, and dangerous bandits.

Once dinner was over, we lingered over cake sweetened with sorghum. "From the look of things in town, Fallow's seen better days," I remarked.

Lawrence nodded. "That it has. The drought's been going for, oh, two years now. We were lucky enough to get some wheat in earlier, but a lot of folk are talking about leaving, and I can't say as I blame them. I don't even remember the last time I saw rain."

I shook my head in sympathy. "I'm sorry to hear it."

"Mr. Harper's farm is doing good, though," he added. "Or your ma's it is legally, I guess."

"Mr. Harper?" Christine inquired.

"My cousin."

"Ruth's brother?" she asked. She and Ruth had gotten on well, the brief times they'd met.

"No." My fork scraped against my plate, cleaning off the last of the cake. "Ruth is from Pa's side of the family. Vernon's mother is Ma's sister. I don't know him well, though we did visit them once in Topeka, when Vernon and I were boys."

Mainly what I recalled of the visit was how Vernon flinched every time his mother raised her voice, even if her words weren't directed at him. He'd been a silent, sullen child, and at the time I'd disliked him for it. Now I understood better, and when Ruth had written with the news he was taking over the farm after Pa's death, I'd been glad for it.

"They have about the only crop worth harvesting right now," Lawrence went on. "Them and the poor farm."

I frowned. "The poor farm?" Odell had been there, for at least a little while. And it sat catty-corner to our—Ma's—farm, on the other side of the fallow place.

Where the Fideles had been drilling.

On the other side of us had been the Walter farm. But I didn't dare ask how it fared. Benjamin had made a life here since I'd left, and I didn't wish to remind anyone of the old scandal.

Would I see him again, this visit? I hadn't when I returned from the asylum, of course. My last glimpse of him had been sun-washed freckles, his brown eyes frightened as the hired hands dragged him in one direction, and me in the other. Pa had shouted at them to take him straight home.

Had he arrived home unscathed? Or had they hurt him, before leaving him on his parents' doorstep? How had his father reacted?

I didn't know. Asking would have only caused more trouble for us both, raised suspicion that there might be something lingering between us. I left town, and he married Marian, and that was all I needed to know.

"Folks are saying the poor farm has a bumper crop this year," Mrs. Reynolds said as she and the boys collected our empty plates. Glad for a distraction, I moved to assist, but she waved me back down. "No, no, don't stir yourself, Mr. Flaherty. I'm sure my Lawrence will have plenty for you to do in the morning."

How long had it been since I'd done this sort of labor? I'd tended horses and occasionally cattle while hunting outlaws in the west, but I'd not set my hand to farm work since leaving for Chicago. "I look forward to it," I said.

Lawrence rose to his feet with a grin. "You say that now. Come on—let's get you fellows settled in the barn for the night. Tomorrow we'll be up with the sun."

CHAPTER 10

Whyborne

"HERE WE ARE," said Mr. Reynolds as he led us into the barn. Christine and Iskander had been offered one of the beds in the small farmhouse, displacing the children who normally slept there to crowd into a cot. Which left the threatened hayloft for Griffin and me. "I'm sorry we can't offer better, Dr. Whyborne."

"That's quite all right," I assured him. "Over the last few years, I've become accustomed to sleeping rough, as they say."

Though I was grateful for the Reynolds' hospitality, I couldn't help but survey our surroundings with a touch of dismay. The two mules who had drawn the wagon stood in the stall nearest the barn doors. The lantern gleamed from the eyes of several cows in other stalls. The air was redolent of hay and manure, and I fought not to wrinkle my nose. What would my clothes smell like in the morning?

"Thank you again, Lawrence," Griffin said.

Mr. Reynolds nodded. "Sleep well. And Griffin…you might want to make sure the doors are secure before you close your eyes. We ain't had any trouble, but there have been rumors."

Griffin frowned. "Rumors?"

"Strange sounds. Prowlers scratching at windows, then running off as soon as anyone calls out. It might be nothing, but folks have taken to locking their doors at night."

"I see. Thank you for the warning." Griffin watched him leave, then made certain of the doors.

"I take it locking one's door is unusual here?" I asked.

"I can't recall it ever happening before." Griffin uneasily shifted the quilts heaped in his arms. "We'd best go up to the loft and make our beds."

I followed him to the rather rickety looking ladder. It creaked and swayed under our combined weight. The need to carry my bedding with me made the climb rather precarious, and I hoped I didn't fall into one of the stalls and end up trampled by a cow.

"I noticed neither of the Reynolds asked why we're staying with them, instead of with your family," I remarked.

Griffin put down his blankets and helped me off the ladder and into the loft itself. "No," he said, his voice carefully neutral. "They didn't. I imagine they can guess well enough."

"Probably." We made a sort of nest amidst the loose hay and spread our blankets within. Tomorrow morning, Griffin would see his mother for the first time since that fateful day in the park back in Widdershins. If not for my connection with the dweller in the deeps, that day might have ended very differently. His parents wouldn't have discovered our relationship. His father wouldn't have forced Griffin to choose between them and me.

"I'm sorry," I said, because I didn't know what else to say. "This entire situation is difficult for you. If there's anything I can do..."

"There isn't." He sank down on the blankets, the hay rustling beneath him. "Other than what you're already doing." He swallowed and looked up at me. "I'm so glad you're here. I can't imagine coming back to Fallow and not having you to rely on."

His words caught me off guard. I would have assumed it far easier to return without me. Surely my presence would only remind his mother of the very reason she'd cut off contact with him in the first place.

I went down to my knees beside him, cupping his face with my scarred right hand. "Of course I'm here, my darling." I kissed him softly. "My husband."

"Make love to me," he whispered against my lips.

We kissed, softly at first, then with more passion. The autumnal chill pricked at my skin as he drew me down to the blankets. "What do you want?" I murmured as his hands unbuttoned my shirt.

His green eyes were wild in the dim light of the kerosene lantern. "Make me feel it," he said. "Whatever happens tomorrow, I want to be reminded of tonight every time I move."

I kissed him again, this time hard enough to feel the imprint of his teeth through his lips. Slipping my thigh between his, I rocked against him, and was rewarded by a growing bulge through the cloth of our trousers.

A part of me wondered if perhaps this was folly. Griffin had been caught in a barn before; making love with him here, our first night in Fallow, might not be the wisest course. But the doors were secured, and we were alone save for the animals and the wind.

And he needed me. I could read his desperation in the way he gripped the back of my neck, the haste with which he undressed when I finally rolled off of him. Whatever tomorrow brought, it wouldn't be easy for him to face. Even the best possible case, that Nella would throw open her arms and welcome him home without reservation, would have its share of pain thanks to the years of silence between them.

I couldn't do anything to take that pain away. But if he found comfort and courage in my body, in the things we did together, I wouldn't deny it to him.

The hay rustled beneath us as we stripped. The lantern light painted his skin in gold, and picked out the first strands of gray in his chestnut hair. I longed to run my hands reverently over his body, to shape every muscle, to kiss and lick every inch.

It wasn't what he needed from me right now, though. He reached for me, and I caught his wrists in my hands, pinning him under me. I kissed him again, then made my way down, biting and sucking the base of his neck while he writhed beneath me.

"You wanted to feel this tomorrow." I slid lower, bit his nipple sharply.

He gasped with pleasure and shock, bucking against me. The tip of his cock left a slick trail over my belly. "Yes, Ival."

"Then roll over."

He did so, a whimper of anticipation escaping him. We'd brought our toiletries with us to the barn, and I searched through them to find the petroleum jelly.

His hands clenched in the blankets in anticipation. He lay on his belly, face turned to the side, eyes shut and lips parted. "Tell me what you're going to do to me," he begged.

He'd always loved to hear me say things to make a sailor blush. I nudged his legs apart and slid a slick finger inside. "I'm going to fuck you," I said breathlessly while he gasped. "Until you beg me to let you come."

His lips curved in a grin half of hunger and half of delight. "Do it."

I grasped his hips, lifting them just high enough from the blanket to give me access. My heart thundered, pulse making my cock jerk slightly, at least until I pushed inside him.

He groaned, an animal sound of pleasure. "Yes. More. Make me feel it."

I gripped his hips hard enough to leave bruises. His body was tight heat, slick and greedy for mine. Our gasps mingled with the sigh of the wind, and a drop of sweat fell from my chin to glisten on the curve of his back. His brows grew tight, teeth bared, fingers tangled in the blankets.

"Feel this," I growled. "Feel me."

"I do. I do, Ival. Oh God."

Pleasure built, the ache sharpening toward something undeniable. "You're going to remember this later," I babbled. "Remember having me; remember being mine."

He cried out suddenly, the friction of the blankets against his member enough to make him spill. His whole body shook beneath me with the force of it, and I bit my lip against a cry of my own as I gave myself over and spent inside him.

After a few long moments while our breathing returned to normal, he rolled over onto his back with a content smile. "Mmm. Thank you, my dear."

I kissed him, gently this time. "My pleasure."

"Not just yours." He reached up and ran his thumb lightly over my cheek. "I love you."

"I love you, too." I reluctantly pulled away. "We should dress before we fall asleep. Just in case."

After we'd dressed, rather than lie down beside me again, Griffin paced to the loft doors, and swung one open a crack. "What are you doing?" I called.

He stared out into the darkness. "It's something we used to do every night. The last thing before going to bed, we'd look out the windows for any sign of light on the horizon."

I sat in the nest of blankets, my elbows resting on my knees. "Light on the horizon?"

"To indicate a distant prairie fire." He folded his arms across his chest and leaned against the door frame. "Fire can wipe out everything in an instant; the trick is to spot one while it's still far enough away to stop it. Or try, anyway."

"Oh." I shifted uncomfortably, trying to find a position where hay didn't poke me through the blankets. I hadn't noticed while distracted by passion, but now I found our bed to be rather uncomfortable. "Do you think you'll see him while we're here? Mr. Walter?"

The loft creaked as Griffin made his way back to me. "Benjamin? I don't know. I hope not. It would only cause trouble for him."

Doubtless he was right. "Do you ever wonder what might have happened if he'd gone to Chicago with you?"

"No." Griffin stretched out by me and rubbed his hand across my back. "He wouldn't have come, and I would never have dared ask it of him."

"I would have," I said. If I'd lived some other life, not bound to a magical vortex. "Gone with you, I mean."

"I know." His hand traced soothing circles. "You've always been braver than I."

"That isn't true," I said quietly. If it had been true, I would have told him everything long before now.

"It is." His certainty hurt. "Now come, my dear. Put out the lantern and lie down. Oh, and Whyborne?"

"Yes?"

"If you have to use the outhouse in the night, do recall the ladder. I'd hate to have you take a step too far and fall on top of the poor cows."

~ * ~

A hellish noise awoke me the next morning—if it could be called morning, when the sun was only evident as a lightening of the eastern sky. I lifted my head groggily, shedding bits of hay that had worked through my blanket and adhered to my hair. Griffin already sat up, brushing hay from his shirt.

The horrid sound repeated itself. "What the devil is that?" I asked.

Griffin turned to me. "Come now, my dear. I know you've heard a rooster crow before, surely."

"Not so accursedly early," I grumbled.

"Did you sleep well?"

"No." Between the hay stabbing me through my blankets and the unfamiliar sounds of the animals drifting from below, I'd waked as much as I'd slept. A dull ache rested behind my eyes, and the world didn't feel quite stable beneath me.

Although the latter might be due as much to my separation from the maelstrom as to lack of sleep. I'd never enjoyed travel. But since I'd first touched the heart of the vortex, trying to keep my blasted Endicott cousins from destroying Widdershins, I found myself physically affected. Traveling meant I felt consistently off, as though in the grip of some mild but very persistent illness. I knew from experience the sensation wouldn't subside until I either returned to Widdershins, or drew close to an arcane line.

"A chance to wash will wake you," Griffin said, picking up a pair of washcloths Lawrence had bundled with our blankets last night. "Leave your coat and vest here—you wouldn't want to spoil them while we do our chores."

"Chores?" I knew he'd spoken of it the night before, but I'd chosen not to dwell on the prospect. "Like…cooking breakfast? Sweeping the front porch?"

Griffin snorted. "Feeding the animals, mucking out the stalls, milking the cows…"

I stopped at the bottom of the ladder to pick yet more hay from my hair. The cows stared at me with their soft eyes. I peered over the side of their stall and glimpsed their swollen, pink udders.

Griffin opened the door and a calico cat wandered in. I crouched down and stroked her head. She purred and arched against my hand. "Is there some task involving cats?" I asked hopefully. "Perhaps she needs brushed." Although she looked sleek enough to my eye.

"She's a barn cat," Griffin said with a smile. "She can look after her own coat. Now come along."

He led the way to the well in the yard. A windmill turned slowly overhead, and he opened the spigot of the pump beneath it to fill a bucket. He tossed a washcloth to me, then unhooked his bracers and unbuttoned his shirt. In moments, he was naked to the waist.

"What on earth are you doing!" I exclaimed.

"Freshening up, of course." Wetting the cloth, he began to scrub enthusiastically at his forearms, face, and chest. When he was done, he bent over and upended the rest of the bucket over his head.

"Your turn," he said, refilling the bucket.

Certainly he didn't expect me to expose myself to the world so casually. Mrs. Reynolds might look out the window and see me, nude to the waist, or someone come by on the road, which ran not far from the yard.

In the end, I compromised by rolling up my sleeves. The water was cold as ice. I splashed it gingerly on my face—I wasn't about to dunk my entire head. Griffin seemed more amused than anything. "We'll make a farmer of you yet."

"Very funny," I muttered.

Reynolds and his three sons emerged from the house. "Chores, breakfast, then school," he was saying to them. Catching sight of Griffin, he added, "Be glad you take lessons in a proper frame house. When we were in school, it was an abandoned soddie that dripped dirty water on our books every time it rained."

Griffin grinned. "And don't forget, we walked uphill both ways."

"In the snow." Reynolds winked. "Since our guests have generously offered to help out with chores this morning, we'll let them choose which they'd prefer."

"Griffin wishes to milk to cows," I said hastily, before he could volunteer me.

Griffin chuckled. "As you like. And what of you, Whyborne?"

"Er..." I hadn't the slightest idea what sorts of chores might be performed at the crack of dawn on a farm.

Dawn. The loud cries of the rooster continued from the coop behind the barn. "Perhaps feed the chickens?" I suggested.

Reynolds looked worried. "Dr. Whyborne, I ought to warn you —"

"Perfect," Griffin said, clapping me on the arm. "You can let them out, fill their water, and scatter feed."

That didn't sound too difficult. "That's what I'll do, then."

Reynolds looked uncertain, but asked his son Simon to show me where everything was kept. Soon enough, I hauled a rather heavy pail of water and a bucket of feed to the henhouse. I refilled the low water trough, then unlatched the henhouse doors and fastened them open.

The hens exited, clucking in excitement when they saw the feed. I scattered some grains for them, and they pecked enthusiastically.

What pleasant animals. Perhaps I could grow to enjoy farm life after all.

The rooster emerged from the henhouse and surveyed me from atop the ramp. He was indeed a handsome specimen, his comb bright red and his tail a sort of iridescent green-black. "Here chick-chick," I coaxed, tossing the grain in his direction.

He fixed me with a yellow eye.

"Yes, here's your breakfast," I said, feeling a bit discomfited by the way the feathers of his neck slowly puffed out.

He started toward me at a walk, ignoring the feed.

"Delicious grain," I said weakly, backing up.

He broke into a run.

I dropped the feed bucket and fled for my life. Wings battered around my waist, and I felt spurs snag in my trousers.

"Griffin!" I shouted. "Griffin, help!"

Griffin came flying out of the barn—then stopped. Rather than come to my aid, he sagged against the door, clutching his stomach and howling with laughter.

"Just hit him with the feed bucket!" Reynolds shouted.

"I dropped it!" I yelled as the infernal creature renewed its assault.

I fled to the front of the house—surely the maddened fowl would abandon pursuit once I left its yard. I caught a glimpse of a gig coming up the lane, but was too busy attempting to defend myself to pay much attention.

"Sorry, Dr. Whyborne!" Simon called as he ran to my aid. He swung a shovel in the general direction of the rooster. "Diablo! Get back!"

The rooster reluctantly broke off. Shaking its feathers, it cast me a look that promised it hadn't yet done with me, then strutted back in the direction of the hens. "Sorry," Simon said again. "Diablo must've thought you were another rooster. He ain't too bright."

"Diablo," I muttered. The thing was well-named, for it was surely Satan incarnate in the form of a harmless chicken.

"Dr. Whyborne?" asked a woman.

I turned and found myself confronted by the occupants of the gig. Three young women, neatly dressed and wearing bright bonnets, stared back at me.

Oh good. At least my humiliation at the hands of a fowl hadn't gone without plenty of witnesses.

"Er, yes." I gave them a small bow. "How may I be of assistance?"

"Please, let me introduce myself," said the blond woman driving the gig. "I'm Miss Martha Tate, and this is Miss Lily Springer, and Miss Dolly Norton."

I nodded stupidly and murmured a greeting. What on earth could they want?

Perhaps seeing my confusion, Miss Tate said, "My mother is the mayor of Fallow, and she heard from a friend at the railroad you'd arrived in town. If only we'd known beforehand, you would have been welcome to stay with us."

"Mr. and Mrs. Reynolds were very kind to offer their hospitality, but thank you," I said.

Miss Springer leaned around Miss Tate to address me. "It is true, ain't it?" she asked breathlessly. "You are the son of the railroad tycoon? And you're here with the lady archaeologist?"

"Er, yes. To both."

All three leaned closer to me at once. It was rather disturbing, like being faced with a pack of hunting wolves. "Mother asked me to extend an invitation to come to dinner tonight," Miss Tate said. "Along with Mr. and Mrs. Barnett, of course."

"Dr. and Mr. Putnam-Barnett," I corrected automatically. Should I accept? Surely the mayor would be in a position to have noticed any suspicious activity on the part of the Fideles.

Unless she was one of them herself.

The invitation hadn't included Griffin. Did they not realize he was here? Or was his exclusion deliberate? Because of the old scandal…or because of whatever had led Odell and Evers to attack him?

He'd wish me to go, though, in case there was any possibility of learning something to our advantage. "Yes," I replied. "We'd be delighted."

"Good," Miss Tate said with a smile. "I look forward to seeing you tonight."

"Do you like pie?" Miss Norton asked.

What an odd question. "Yes?"

"My strawberry pie won first place at the fair," Miss Norton stated proudly. "Of course, strawberries are out of season now, but my pumpkin is even better. I'll bring you a pie and you can taste for yourself."

"Oh. Er, thank you," I said. "I'd best, um, get back to...things."

"Of course." Miss Tate straightened and snapped the reins. Within moments, the gig rumbled off, leaving a cloud of dust in its wake.

The farmhouse door opened, and Christine stepped out. "What a bunch of sharks," she observed.

"Whatever do you mean?"

She gave me a pitying look. "Honestly, Whyborne, they were all three eyeing you up like a prize cut of beef. Due to your fortune, naturally, not your looks." Before I could object, she said, "Well, best you'd come inside. Mrs. Reynolds has breakfast ready." She wrinkled her nose. "And good heavens, man, wash up first! You smell like a cow."

~ * ~

"It's so...large," I said.

Of course I'd glimpsed the plains on our way from the town yesterday, but nightfall had kept me from truly appreciating their vastness. Intellectually I'd known the plains were flat, but I was unprepared for the expanse of endless earth stretching out before me. There were no hills to block the view, only distant farmhouses, barns, or windmills, widely scattered amidst a sea of brown, withered corn stalks. The road ran perfectly straight, intersecting other roads at precise ninety-degree angles, as neatly as a grid. It seemed a strange, lonely place to my eyes.

Lawrence had lent us the wagon and mules. Griffin drove, while Christine sat beside him, and Iskander and I rode in the back. A huge cloud of dust billowed up as we made our way down the unnaturally straight road, and within half a mile Iskander and I were utterly covered with a pale brown film.

"This is worse than the sandstorm in Egypt," I said, brushing at it futilely.

"I hate seeing this," Griffin said. "Look at it—the corn should be ten feet tall and in the midst of being harvested."

Most of the stalks around us would barely reach my knee, and there was no sign of anything I'd call a harvest taking place. Every gust of the wind bore on it a fine haze of yet more dust, lifted from the dry, desiccated earth of the fields.

"No wonder the town is dying," Christine remarked.

Griffin shook his head. "Farming is a hard, uncertain life," he said. "The first year I lived here, everything had been going well. Crops were flourishing. Then the grasshoppers came."

"Grasshoppers?" Iskander asked.

"So many they blotted out the sun."

I looked up at the vast sky; it seemed impossible to imagine that many insects. "And they ate the crops?"

"They ate *everything*. Fruits, vegetables, wheat, corn. We put burlap sacks over the garden to keep them off, but they simply ate the sacks first. Paper, tree bark, the wooden handles of our tools, even our clothes if we went outside in the thick of them. Their bodies spoiled any water left uncovered. Only the chickens were happy—they gorged themselves silly. But the grasshoppers had some secretion or oil that spoiled their flesh. The few chickens we slaughtered tasted too awful to eat."

I tried to imagine such devastation. "That's terrible."

"We made it through, though." Griffin stared off across the fields. "Pa said we had to put our faith in God. We prayed together every night and every morning, and if he ever doubted the Creator would fail us, he never showed it. And eventually the grasshoppers left. Rail cars came from the east, carrying the food we needed to survive, and enough grain to plant for the next year."

"But wouldn't God have created the grasshoppers as well?" Christine asked dubiously.

"Christine, please," Iskander said.

"I'm only saying—"

"Yes, dearest, we know what you're saying."

Griffin stiffened suddenly and pointed. "There's an arcane line! It must be the same one we crossed over before coming into town. I never imagined there was one so close to the farm."

My heart plummeted and my palms grew damp. Of course there was a line. It made sense, didn't it? How else was the damnable maelstrom to exert its will on the unwary?

Griffin had lived here his entire childhood, unaware of the arcane magic flowing through the earth. He'd escaped to Chicago without it harming him...and then returned, marked by the umbra, to be collected.

God.

"Fascinating." Christine peered in the direction Griffin pointed, as though she might suddenly perceive it as well. "I do wish we knew more about these arcane lines. Do they all connect in some fashion? If we followed this one, would it eventually lead us to Widdershins?"

"I don't know," I said. "It hardly matters, at any rate."

It did matter, of course. Very much.

Iskander had risen to his knees to look as well. Now a frown creased his brown brow. "I say, is that…green?"

As we drew closer, it became apparent he was right. In contrast to the withered fields we'd passed through, those on the horizon appeared to be thriving.

"Mr. Reynolds did say the farm was doing well," Christine said with a frown. "But this is more of a contrast than I'd expected."

Even from a distance, the difference could not have been more stark. The fields we'd passed had only withered brown and yellow stalks, stunted to knee height at best. But the Kerr fields boasted a literal wall of green, towering far overhead, save where the harvest had already removed stalks heavy with ripened corn.

"There's the house," Griffin said, indicating a structure at the edge of the verdant fields. Then a deep frown suddenly creased his face. "That windmill—not the one near the house, but further back. It wasn't there before."

"I imagine much will have changed in the four years since you left," I said sympathetically.

He made a negating motion. "It isn't that. It's the windmill's location. Perhaps I'm wrong, but I think it must be near the fallow spot, if not in it."

"Bloody hell," Iskander said, sitting back. "The drilling equipment in the photographs. Could the Fideles have been seeking artifacts of the masters under the guise of drilling new wells to combat the drought?"

"There's a second one." Griffin pointed. "If I remember where the boundaries were, it's near the poor farm." Fear sparked in his eyes. "Do you think the water could have some sort of contamination?"

"I doubt it," I said dubiously. "It seems clear from the writing on the photo that the Fideles were looking for the transferal sphere. Whatever the sphere's original purpose, it seems innocuous enough now. And if the water was contaminated, surely the crops wouldn't be thriving as they are."

A mailbox sat on a post to one side of the dusty road. Griffin halted the mules beside it and stared down the track leading to a large farmhouse. Wash flapped on the line to one side, and a weathered windmill turned slowly near a barn.

"Is this it?" I asked. He nodded.

I studied it with a new eye. This was where he'd grown to manhood. The place that had shaped him, as Widdershins had shaped me.

Well. Not so literally in his case, I assumed.

"Should one of us come with you?" I couldn't imagine what he must feel at the moment. His mother, whom he hadn't seen for three years, was likely in that very house. Would he wish to confront her alone, or with someone at his side?

"Someone ought to," Christine said. "Griffin's already been attacked twice."

"No." He straightened his shoulders. "I'll be fine. And if for some reason I'm not, I have my revolver with me. If you hear me fire a shot, take it as a signal for help."

I didn't like it, but I nodded. "As you wish."

"In the meantime, why don't the rest of you inspect the area where the artifact was found?" he suggested. "As Iskander suggested, the windmill must be on the very spot. You can cut through the corn field to get there."

I didn't like leaving him to face Nella alone…but my presence would hardly help the situation. "All right."

Griffin passed the reins to Christine. "I'll join you at the well in the fallow spot," he said, swinging down from the driver's seat.

I caught his hand. "Griffin…"

He cast me a smile. "Don't worry, my dear. I assure you, last night you gave me something to remember you by today, even while we're apart."

I blushed furiously. Iskander looked fixedly away, but Christine laughed aloud.

"There you have it," she said, and urged the mules forward. I glanced back in Griffin's direction, but his form had already been lost behind a cloud of dust.

CHAPTER 11

Griffin

I WALKED SLOWLY up the lane to the house, my heart pounding in my throat. The structure sported a fresh coat of bright, white paint. The warm sunlight beat down on me, and every step stirred up dust from the rutted lane. In the distance, the corn field created a wall of green stretching off in the direction of the fallow spot.

I'd grown up believing the barren place cursed. We didn't plant the corn too close, even though it meant leaving a strip of empty land between the fallow place and our crop. No one would risk putting a well there, lest whatever unknown poison kept anything from growing in the spot leech into the water.

Ma must have been desperate to let anyone drill there for water, let alone use it to irrigate the crops.

The farm seemed unnaturally silent as I walked up to the house. There came no barking of dogs. No cluck of chickens. Not even the meow of a barn cat come to investigate the new arrival.

We'd always had dogs to chase away predators, or hunt prairie chickens, or warn of visitors. And of course we kept a healthy clowder to keep the mice out of the grain. Even if Vernon had decided against raising chickens for eggs or cows for milk, he'd surely have kept the dogs and cats.

So where were they?

Movement caught my attention. A woman made for the small garden meant to provide vegetables for the house. Although she was too far away for me to make out her face beneath her bonnet, her posture straightened when she spotted me. Before I could call a greeting, she turned and ran in the direction of the fields.

No doubt she meant to fetch the men of the household. Lawrence had spoken of prowlers—perhaps she deemed it better to be safe than sorry.

Then the front door opened, and I forgot all about her when Ma stepped out on the porch.

More lines of care lay on Ma's face than when I'd last seen her. We'd been in the park in Widdershins, with Whyborne and my cousin Ruth. I'd spent the visit keeping alive my parents' hope I might marry Ruth. So as not to disappoint them too prematurely, I'd invited her for a carriage ride around the park.

I'd been an idiot, asking Ival to come to such an outing, forcing him to watch me pretend to court Ruth. I'd stupidly assumed he'd know it was all a sham—and that, even knowing, it wouldn't break his heart.

Then cultists had attacked us, and the fact that I'd been lying about our living arrangements came to light. Pa ordered Ma and Ruth back to the hotel, and I'd been so frantic over Whyborne I hadn't even thought to look at Ma. To get one last glimpse of her face.

I blinked, and the arcane line glowed faintly in the distance in my shadowsight, cutting a path through the fields and curving not far from the house. But Ma...

She was just an old woman. No sign of corruption on her skin at all, and I half wanted to collapse with the relief of it.

"Griffin?" she whispered, and sagged against the doorframe. News of our arrival might have spread to folk in the town like the mayor, but it clearly hadn't yet reached the far flung houses.

"Hello, Ma." I wanted to say more, but my throat constricted impossibly. I came to a halt at the bottom of the porch steps, unsure of my welcome.

She put a hand to the bodice of the faded gingham dress she wore.

"Has something happened to Ruth?"

"No." I chanced the steps. I ached to hug her, to feel her arms go around me, but she didn't move from the doorway. "Ruth is fine. Can I...can I come in?"

Hope sparked in her eyes. "Oh, Griffin...have you come back to us?"

It seemed an odd way to put it. "I never wanted to leave."

Tears spilled down her cheeks, and she finally embraced me. I returned the hug, holding her tight. She felt so frail, hollowed out by the slow weight of years and the hard life of a farmer's wife. I breathed deep and smelled baking bread and dried lavender, and my heart ached with the familiarity of it all.

Eventually, she pulled back and wiped her eyes with the corner of her apron. "Look at me, being all silly," she said with a little laugh. "Come in. You must be hungry—I'll get you some biscuits and a bit of sausage to hold you until lunch."

The house seemed so much smaller than it had before. A lump formed in my throat at the sight of Pa's old chair in the sitting room, the table and chairs Ma proudly ordered from a catalog, the worn spinning wheel she'd spent so many nights working while Pa read to us from the Bible.

I followed her to the kitchen. "Sit down; sit down," Ma said, ushering me to the table. "I'll just get that biscuit."

How many times had I sat here as a child, eating what she cooked for me? Biscuits and eggs, beans cooked with pork fat, bread with fresh churned butter. An apple pie every year on my birthday.

Tears threatened, and I fought against them. If I'd come here to find her corrupted by some horrible magic...but I hadn't.

And she hadn't turned me away, but brought me inside. Welcomed me home. The only thing that could have made this moment better would have been if Pa were alive.

"I'm so glad you've come back," she said, tears choking her voice. She put a biscuit, no doubt left over from breakfast, on a plate along with the promised sausage.

"So am I." I caught her hand when she set the plate in front of me. "Sit down. Let me talk to you."

She swallowed thickly and nodded. "Just let me pour us some coffee, then."

I took a bite of the biscuit, washed it down with the coffee. "You remembered how I take my coffee," I said.

"Of course I do." She sat beside me, looking at me as though she couldn't believe I was here. "You're my son."

Had she feared I was angry with her? Had she only been waiting for my return, afraid to reach out first after my falling out with Pa? "I've missed you, too," I said.

She gave me a tearful smile. "Oh, Griffin, I prayed this day would come. God has truly smiled on this family. First the harvest, and now you."

A thread of unease touched me, but I pushed it away. "I saw the fields, though only in the distance. It appears you've escaped the ravages of the drought."

"I should've known it was a sign." She glanced at the cross hanging on the wall and smiled. "The drought was awful. Our corn looked as bad as the rest. But then Vernon had the idea of putting in the new well—and to think I tried to talk him out of it!"

"Why?"

She laughed, as if amused by her former self. "Foolishness. He wanted to put it in the fallow place, and I told him no, the earth there is poison. But he insisted."

Vernon had the idea...or had the Fideles put it in his head? They would have needed someone's permission to drill on the property, after all. "What happened?"

"A miracle." Her eyes shone. "Within days—hours—the corn had completely revived. Green and growing faster than I've ever seen it in all my years. It should have been too late in the season for it to flourish the way it did, but...well, see for yourself! We're going to have a bumper crop." She glanced again at the cross. "Vernon put his faith in God's inspiration, ignored my doubt, and was rewarded."

"I'm sure you're right," I said, though I wasn't certain of it at all. The artifact from the well had been some creation of the masters. Perhaps whatever deep aquifer it came from had some ancient sorcery laid on it, to make the water more nourishing than ordinary. If so, at least for once the masters' spells seemed to be doing good rather than harm.

"Our prayers were answered once," she said. "And now mine have been again. Oh Griffin—after what your Pa said you'd done—I never thought you'd return. I should have had faith that God would change your heart and lead you away from a path of sin."

Realization crashed down over me. She thought I'd returned for good. Given up my life in Widdershins, given up men.

Given up my Ival.

"Marian won't be too pleased at first," she was saying, "but she'll come around. Just give her time. This will be a new beginning for us all."

"Ma, I'm not—"

Through the open window drifted the sound of Whyborne shouting my name.

CHAPTER 12

Whyborne

"WHAT THE DEVIL is wrong with these mules?" Christine grumbled.

She'd driven the wagon farther down the road, to a point where the corn grew almost to the dusty track. Part of the field had been cut already; in the distance, men guided some sort of steam driven harvesting machine. As we drew closer to the remaining wall of green stalks, the mules began to slow, ignoring the flick of the reins. Now they tossed their heads, and one seemed to be attempting to back up in its traces.

"Something must have frightened them," Iskander said, baffled.

"Wolves?" I hazarded. "Are there wolves here?"

"This close to town?" Iskander seemed dubious.

I looked at the emptiness all around us, save for the scattered farmhouses. "It isn't that close."

"Whatever has them spooked, we don't have time for it," Christine replied. "We need to take a look at the area around the well, and do so quickly, in case Griffin's mother decides she doesn't want the likes of us on her property."

I very much hoped Christine was wrong, for Griffin's sake. Even if Nella would never approve of my presence in his life, perhaps she could at least unbend enough to renew their relationship.

Then I'd tell him the truth, and he would stay here, in Fallow. Safe, or at least safer. And I'd go home alone.

We tied the unhappy mules to the fence, before climbing over and into the field. "We should walk along the irrigation channel," Iskander said, indicating a long, low ditch filled with water. It ran between walls of tall, green corn, each stalk burgeoning with tasseled ears. "That way we won't disturb the corn."

"And it will keep us out of sight of the harvesters," Christine agreed.

The air immediately cooled as we entered the field. The smell of green sap and damp earth saturated my lungs with every breath, so very different from the fish and salt of home.

Iskander dropped back to walk with me while Christine strode ahead. "I know this must be difficult for you," he said in a low voice. "When Christine's parents disowned her for marrying me, I couldn't help but feel, well, guilty."

I winced. "I imagine that was quite the family visit." Christine had brought Iskander to Philadelphia to meet her parents, without first mentioning to them that he was half Egyptian. The color of his skin had not met with their approval.

"I've never seen Christine so angry," Iskander agreed. "She and her mother are much alike in temperament—although good heavens, don't tell her I said so! Her mother had been, ah, imbibing. Things went very wrong very quickly."

"I'm so sorry."

"No, no." Iskander waved me off. "I only mean to say I sympathize with your situation. It isn't easy knowing you cost the one you love most in the world their family."

I'd cost Christine a great deal more than that, assuming the maelstrom had collected her. And why wouldn't it have chosen the most brilliant archaeologist in a generation?

"Yes," I said quietly. "It isn't easy at all."

The field seemed to stretch on endlessly. Sweat beaded on my brow, and I took off my hat periodically to fan myself. At least there didn't seem to be any insects about. I considered wetting my handkerchief with water from the irrigation ditch and wiping some of the dust and sweat off, but the return trip would only get me filthy again.

When the end to the corn came, it was surprisingly abrupt. We stepped out from amidst the stalks and found ourselves on the edge of a wide, barren patch, several acres in size. Though corn crowded in all around it, not a single stalk sprouted within its irregular confines. Not even the heartiest weeds had found a home amidst the cracked, barren earth. Every puff of wind raised a dust devil, and the nearest stalks were coated in a fine layer of brown.

I stepped out onto the arid ground. Instantly, the faint feeling of weakness I'd had since leaving Widdershins vanished. "The arcane line runs through here."

Christine joined me. "Do you think it has any connection with the fact nothing will grow?"

"I can't imagine it would. It surely must run for miles—Griffin said he saw it even before we arrived."

Iskander looked around. "How should we proceed, Christine? If nothing else, years of agriculture have disrupted the site rather badly."

We'd agreed to treat our search for any sign of what the masters might have left here—and the Fideles after—as part of an archaeological dig. For one, it would lend credence to our cover story, should anyone question us. For another, Christine's methods would allow us to survey the area for any remaining traces of the masters' presence.

"We'll walk a few transects, radiating out from the well and into the fields," she decided. "Whyborne, we're looking for any sign of an old disturbance. Changes in soil color, where a structure might once have stood before rotting into the ground. Any fragment turned up by the plow that might be part of an artifact. A pattern in the corn where it isn't as tall as the surrounding stalks, which might indicate a buried structure beneath. Once we're done, Griffin will have hopefully secured permission for us to be here, and we'll investigate the barren spot as well."

"If the sphere came from so far below the ground, will we see anything at the surface?" I asked dubiously.

"Possibly not," she admitted. "But we can't rule it out."

We did as she ordered. I soon found myself making my way between rows of corn. Had there once been a city here, similar to the city of shadows in Alaska? Its walls destroyed by the relentless forces of water and wind, worn away and buried, until nothing remained?

Or had the sphere come to be here in some completely different fashion? Had it been deliberately buried deep in the earth?

The sphere had been burned out from the inside, according to Christine. What had once lurked inside, ready to burst free? And where had it gone after? The Fideles had clearly been searching for something, so presumably whatever was originally inside the sphere hadn't gone far.

Perhaps not far at all. They'd confined their search to the fallow spot, which suggested they might have an idea as to what caused it in the first place.

I shook my head and forced myself to focus on the task at hand. The irrigation ditch had cut a wide path, but now that I was edging through the rows themselves, I felt curiously claustrophobic. Green stalks hemmed me in on either side, their leaves whispering in the breeze.

I didn't feel a breeze.

I came to a halt, listening intently. Were the leaves rustling…or whispering?

A soft moan sounded to my left.

I spun, my heart rabbiting in my chest. I peered through the stalks, but could see nothing save endless rows of corn. "Who's there?" I called.

There came no answer…but the rustling increased. As if something moved through the corn toward me.

I swallowed hard. It could be anything. Wouldn't I feel the fool if it turned out to be a stray cow?

God, I hoped it was a stray cow. Even a murderous rooster.

"Who the hell are you?" growled an angry voice behind me.

~ * ~

I let out a startled cry. A man stood behind me, his handsome face drawn into angry lines. His clothing was covered in dirt and bits of corn husk, and he carried a heavy knife.

I held up my hands quickly. "Please, allow me to explain."

He stalked toward me, expression menacing. "You ain't from around here. Who are you? What do you want?"

"M-My name is Dr. Percival Endicott Whyborne," I said, backing up quickly as he continued to approach. "I'm here with the Nathaniel R. Ladysmith museum. An artifact was found on this land, and we came to see—just to look—"

His expression failed to get any friendlier. "We don't appreciate trespassers here."

"We aren't!" I lied. "One of my companions is the son of the woman who owns the farm."

The man's eyes widened, and his grip tightened on the knife. "Griffin Flaherty?" he demanded. "Is that who you mean?"

Curse it. Griffin had already been attacked twice already. Why had I been so quick to invoke his name?

"Yes?" I said uncertainly.

The man shoved his way through the stalks into the next row and broke into a run, heading in the direction of the house.

Panic seized me—surely the man must be corrupted, just as Odell and Evers had been. I bolted after him, shouting for Christine and Iskander at the top of my lungs. My mind raced—should I use sorcery to stop him before he reached the house and Griffin? Risk flattening the crops with a burst of wind? But that would destroy the harvest, and Griffin surely wouldn't thank me for leaving his mother destitute. Fire was out for the same reason, and the water of the irrigation ditch was too far away to be of use.

Blast it.

My side was burning by the time I reached the end of the fields. A wide area of dry ground lay between fields and house, occupied by a barn and a few empty pens, which must have held livestock at one time. A woman had joined the man, and together they ran for the back door.

"Griffin!" I shouted. "Griffin!"

"Whyborne!" Christine bellowed from behind me. "What's going on?"

I hadn't the time or the breath to tell her. She and Iskander caught up with me just as I reached the back door, which stood open.

"Vernon!" exclaimed a voice I recognized as Nella Kerr's. "What do you think you're doing?"

"How dare you show your face here?" Vernon said. "How dare you come among decent folk, and sit at our table, and—"

I stumbled into the room and came to a halt. Vernon stood nearest me. A woman I assumed to be his wife held onto his arm, a furious glare fixed on Griffin. Nella Kerr and Griffin both stood at the table, their chairs pushed back and a half-eaten biscuit on a plate between them. Griffin's skin had gone pale, freckles standing out, and his jaw was clenched.

Nella let out a gasp at the sight of me. She put a hand to her chest and her gaze darted from me to Griffin. "You brought *him* with you?"

The younger woman turned to me—then took a quick step back. "Who are you?" she demanded.

Between the dust and sweat, I must look like a madman, if my appearance alarmed her so. "Let me explain," I said to the room in general, although what explanation I could possibly give I didn't know.

"We're here on an archaeological expedition," Christine said quickly. "An artifact was found in your field, and—"

Mrs. Kerr ignored us both. "I thought you'd come back," she said to Griffin. "I thought God answered my prayers, brought you into the light." She glanced at me again. "I thought I'd been forgiven."

The younger woman continued to stare at me as though I were a snake let loose in her kitchen. "You aren't welcome here." She turned her glare back to Griffin. "And you. You'll pay for what you did."

Oh God. The same words as the corrupted men had spoken to him in Widdershins.

I cast a wild glance at him, but his gaze was locked on her, his eyes wide with horror. "Marian?" Griffin looked shocked to see her. "Ma said...but Benjamin...?"

"How dare you speak his name?" Marian snarled.

"I think Aunt Nella and my wife have made themselves clear." Vernon's voice was cold and hard as stone. "And so have I. Leave this house and don't come back. Ever."

Christine held up a restraining hand. "Actually, I was hoping to get your permission to conduct an archaeological survey on your land. As I said—"

"Out!"

"How rude!" she said with a sniff.

"We'll just be leaving," Iskander said with a wary glance at the knife. He caught Christine by the elbow and steered her toward the front door.

I wanted to protest, but there was nothing to be said. When we reached the door, Griffin paused. "We'll be at the Reynolds' farm for at least a few more days, Ma. If you want to talk."

Nella sank down and put her face in her hands. Marian shot me a venomous look, then turned her gaze on Griffin, with such an expression of raw hate it took me aback. "You're going to be sorry you came back to Fallow, Griffin. As sorry as I can make you."

Griffin looked as though he wished to argue. But instead, he simply nodded, and followed the rest of us out of the house.

CHAPTER 13

Griffin

"I'm sorry," **Whyborne** said, once we were well away.

Christine had taken up the reins, and Iskander sat in the front of the wagon beside her. Glad not to have to think, I climbed into the back beside Whyborne. We sat without touching, watching the farm recede into the distance behind us.

I'd hoped. For a few moments, I'd truly believed Ma had wanted me back, despite everything.

She'd hoped, too. For a few moments, she'd believed I'd changed. Repented. Left the man I loved above all others and returned to become the son she wanted me to be.

"I thought I'd been forgiven." What did she mean by that? Did she blame herself for my attraction to men, believe she'd made some error in raising me?

I ached to fall into Ival's arms. To have him wrapped around me, so I could breathe in his scent, feel his fingers stroke my hair, listen to him murmur that he loved me.

But we were on a public road in the middle of the day. So I only said, "You have nothing to apologize for, my dear."

"You're better off without them in my opinion," Christine declared.

"Christine," Iskander said. "You aren't helping matters."

"I only mean to say Griffin is worth more than the whole lot of them put together."

My very bones ached with loss. But there were more important matters at hand than my bruised feelings. "Ma wasn't corrupted, nor was Vernon." I paused, remembering her rage. "Marian is."

"I heard what she said. The same words as the other corrupted spoke." Ival looked at me uncertainly. "She's Vernon's wife?"

"So it would seem. Which…I don't understand." I stared down at my hands in my lap. At the white pearl set in my wedding ring. "Marian married Benjamin, after I left for Chicago. I was run out of town, but as he and Marian were already engaged, the wedding was hastily moved up. It was meant to demonstrate he was a changed man. Ma made sure to tell me about it, in one of the first letters she sent. Probably to make certain I wasn't tempted to come back for him. Or maybe to keep me from hoping he'd join me, I don't know." I swallowed. "If Benjamin is dead…"

"Perhaps they were divorced?" Christine suggested hopefully.

"It is possible," I allowed. "The divorce laws in Kansas are quite liberal." I shook my head. Whatever had become of Benjamin, I couldn't worry about him at the moment. "How Marian and Vernon, or even Ma, feel about me doesn't matter. Marian is corrupted, which means they're all in danger."

"Do you think she's a member of the Fideles, then?" Whyborne asked. "Like Odell and Evers?"

"I've no idea." It didn't make sense, or at least, no more sense than a man like Odell joining the cult. But the photos proved the Fideles had dug the new well; they would have had a chance to speak with her. To offer her…what?

"If only we knew what this corruption even is." Whyborne took out his handkerchief and wiped some of the dust from his face. "Or why the corrupted seem so fixated on you, Griffin."

"At least Marian didn't physically assault him," Iskander pointed out.

"All I can say is that it's extraordinarily strange not to be the one everyone wants to kill." Whyborne folded his handkerchief and put it back in his pocket. "If Griffin wasn't in danger, I'd almost call it a pleasant change of pace."

"Well, it's only fair we should take turns with this sort of thing," I said. "Did you find anything in the field? Any clue?"

"Not a blasted thing," Christine groused. "Kander?"

He shook his head. "Nothing. Though we didn't have much time to look."

Whyborne shivered. "I…I thought I heard something in the corn. Like the rustle of a breeze, except I didn't feel any stirring of air. Whether it was a trick of the wind or something else, a moment later I'm certain I heard a moan. And there was something moving among the rows."

"A stray farm animal?" Iskander suggested hopefully.

"There wasn't any livestock," I recalled. "No dogs. No barn cats. Not even any chickens."

"Thank heavens for small favors," Whyborne muttered. "I don't know what it was. Before I could investigate, Vernon appeared and started waving around his knife and threatening me. He must have spotted us and thought us trespassers. Mr. Reynolds spoke of nocturnal prowlers going about frightening people—perhaps Vernon believed us the culprits. I rather thought I might have to defend myself against him, truth be told. Until he realized we were with you, Griffin, and… well." Whyborne glanced worriedly at me. "I thought he meant to kill you. You're certain he wasn't corrupted?"

It made no sense. Even if Vernon had believed them indigent trespassers, he would have seen Christine with them. The presence of a woman should have soothed his fears, or at least caused him to approach less aggressively.

Not to mention he apparently hadn't brought any field hands with him. If he believed he'd spotted a group of potentially dangerous prowlers, why not take the rest of the work crew to apprehend them?

"His animosity for me aside, I find Vernon's action suspicious," I said carefully. "Although I suppose I might be letting personal sentiment cloud my judgment."

"Do you think he's hiding something?" Iskander asked. "But what? And if his own wife is corrupted, yet he isn't…well, I'm not certain what that could mean. Is he a Fideles? Or is she hiding secrets from him?"

"I've no idea." I stared out over the bleak fields of dead, stunted corn. Many farms would be abandoned after such a harsh year, and their former inhabitants find themselves destitute on the poor farm. "We need to find out what this corruption is."

"Perhaps we'll learn something at this blasted dinner with the mayor," Christine said. "Although I'm not even certain what questions to ask at this point. I suppose 'Pardon me, do you belong to any murderous cults?' is out."

"You might need a bit more subtlety than that," I agreed. For a moment, I considered going with them, even though I hadn't been invited. Surely the mayor wouldn't just throw me out if I turned up on her doorstep.

But I had questions of my own, which Lawrence could answer. Starting with what exactly had become of Benjamin Walter.

~ * ~

That evening, Whyborne, Iskander, and Christine borrowed the Reynolds' wagon yet again, to take them to the mayor's house. Having no wish to add to Annie's chores, I'd pressed Whyborne's suit while he scrubbed off as much of the road dust as possible. By the time he drove off, he looked quite respectable, with his hair tamed by oil and a bit of cologne to cover the smell of livestock. No doubt the young ladies at the dinner would appreciate my efforts.

"The mayor didn't invite you," Simon observed from the doorway as I watched them drive away.

"I'm not rich or famous enough to be interesting," I replied lightly. And possibly it was even true. Surely not everyone in Fallow knew of the old scandal, or recalled it after all this time. Perhaps Mayor Tate thought me Whyborne's secretary or servant, if she knew of my existence at all.

"Ma's a better cook anyway," Simon said loyally. "She said to wash up and come in for dinner."

When we sat down to our meal, Annie asked, "Would you like to say grace tonight, Griffin?"

It had been a long time since I'd spoken grace over a meal. Whyborne was a thoroughgoing atheist, but I couldn't blame my lapse on him. I'd long ago fallen out of the habit, just as I'd ceased to say a nightly prayer years before we'd met.

I clasped my hands and bowed my head. What to say? "Heavenly Father, we thank you for this meal. For the good earth that provided it, and the sun and rain which came in their due time." I licked the memory of dust from my lips. "And I pray You continue to provide for this community. Keep all within it safe and whole. Amen."

After dinner, Lawrence invited me to sit in front of the fire with him. The October nights held a chill, even this early in the month, and I was glad to agree. He took out a corncob pipe and set about packing and lighting it. His wife settled their children with books and toys, before retreating to a comfortable chair and taking up her sewing.

A nostalgic ache started in my chest. Pa and I had sat like this many an evening, after a long day of work in the fields. Only the laughter of children was different. Pa had built a big house, expecting to fill it with offspring. But that particular blessing had never come, and I'd been the only child they chose to adopt.

Did Vernon and Marian have any children? Or did she have any from her marriage to Benjamin?

The memory of corruption on her face caused me to shudder. God, I hoped not. If this was some kind of magical infection or sickness, if it couldn't be cured…

"You were right about Vernon's crop being almost the only one left worth harvesting," I said to Lawrence. "Theirs and the poor farm's."

Lawrence blew a long stream of fragrant smoke from his nostrils. "Should I ask how your ma is doing?"

I looked away. "Well enough, as far as I can tell."

"You know, folks claimed marrying my Annie was a sin," Lawrence said, his voice pitched so low I could barely hear it above the crackle of the fire. "Quoting Deuteronomy at me, about how God divided the nations and separated the sons of Adam. Saying the mingling of races is what brought about the great flood."

And we Sodomites were only blamed for destroying a city or two. "I'm sorry," I said.

He shook his head. "I'm just saying what is. Folks are so quick to cast the first stone. They forget the bit about not judging lest ye be judged."

"Things didn't go well with Ma, as you've guessed," I admitted. "Or Vernon. But the one who seemed the most upset to see me was Marian, truth be told." I hesitated. "I was shocked to see her there. Did she and Benjamin get divorced, or…?"

"Aw, heck, you didn't know?" Lawrence's eyes widened. "I didn't mention it last night, because I figured your ma had told you."

"Then he's dead," I said, the last bit of hope I'd clung to disintegrating.

"I'm afraid so." Lawrence sank back in his chair. "It happened a few years after you left. Marian went out looking for him when he was late for supper. She found him in the barn, shot through the head and with a gun in his hand."

I could still remember the spray of freckles that the sun brought out on his face. Running footraces down the road on Sunday afternoons. The nervous flutter in my belly the first time we'd kissed. The desperation burning in every fiber of my being when he'd told me to unfasten my trousers and bend over for him.

A few moments of pleasure to blot out years of pain and fear, of knowing something was wrong with me, of praying it could be changed.

"May God have mercy on his soul," I said through numb lips.

"Amen." Lawrence leaned forward and tapped out the ashes from his pipe against the hearth. "It was suicide, though Marian called it murder, so Parson Norton refused to let him be buried in the churchyard."

"Murder?"

Lawrence rubbed tiredly at his eyes. "Not directly, but talk about him never really died down, even after you left. Marian claimed somebody sent Benjamin anonymous letters every month, calling him a sinner, telling him he was bound for hell for what he'd done. Once or twice a year, the newspaper would print anonymous letters sent to them, railing against letting him stay in Fallow. Of course that damned —pardon me—editor Carson printed them, and was happy to do it."

"God." I'd never known. Never guessed.

My departure was supposed to fix things for him. Instead, I felt as though I'd abandoned Benjamin to his death.

"Maybe if he and Marian had children, things would have been different." Lawrence glanced at Simon, head bent studiously over a book in the dim light of the kerosene lantern. "Then again, maybe not."

"What was that?" Annie asked, looking up from her sewing. "I thought I heard something outside."

The house fell silent, save for the crackle of the fire, the low creak of the beams in the wind. Just as I began to think she'd imagined it, there came a low scratching noise from beneath one of the windows.

"Must be the dogs," Lawrence said uneasily. He rose to his feet, checked that his shotgun was in easy reach, and opened the door.

Two dogs raced inside, their ears back and their tails tucked between their legs. They cowered beneath the table, eyes fixed on the open door, clearly too terrified even to bark.

I drew out my revolver. "Something is out there."

Lawrence picked up the shotgun. "Don't worry," he told Annie. "Probably a wolf spooked them."

But he didn't sound as if he believed it.

Annie pulled her children close, but her eyes remained fixed on her husband. "Maybe you ought to stay inside."

"This ain't Alabama," he said. "If it's a wolf we'll scare it off, and if it's prowlers, we'll send them running too. You just stay here. We'll be right back."

I took up a lantern, and we stepped out onto the porch, shutting the door behind us. Night had fallen, the sky distinguishable from the plains only by the presence of stars.

The yard was empty, at least within the reach of our lantern light. "No horses," Lawrence murmured, and I recalled his comment about Alabama. Annie's family no doubt had brought with them dark tales of riders in the night.

Lawrence led the way around the side of the house, where we'd heard the scratching. I held the lantern high, directing its light along the wall.

"Nothing here," he said, but I heard the unease in his voice. "If it was a wolf, maybe we scared it—"

There came the sound of running footsteps, and a heavy body slammed into me.

CHAPTER 14

Whyborne

"I'M SO PLEASED you could come, Dr. Putnam. That is, Dr. Putnam-Barnett," said Mayor Tate. "And your husband and Dr. Whyborne, of course."

The Tate house was the largest within the town proper. Mr. Tate, a big man with a generous belly, greeted us as warmly as his wife. Miss Tate was naturally present for the dinner party, as was Miss Norton. I bowed politely over their hands. Both of them smiled and blinked their eyes a great deal in my direction.

"And this is Parson Norton, Miss Norton's father," Mayor Tate went on.

Parson Norton had thinning gray hair and a rather red face. "I look forward to seeing you in church Sunday morning," he said as we shook hands. I muttered something vague in reply.

"I'm glad to report we'll be giving Whyborne Railroad and Industries our business in a few days, once the harvest is finished," Mr. Tate said, once introductions were finished. "Folks here need some hope, and the sight of your train cars stuffed with our corn, heading to

Widdershins, will uplift many a heart."

Dear lord, I hoped the man didn't intend to talk business throughout the evening. I hadn't the slightest interest in Father's empire. "I saw the grain elevators when we arrived on the train."

His chest puffed out slightly. "I own those—or a share in them, anyway. The old grain company no longer believed in our little town, closed up operations, and moved on. Fortunately Loyal Grain showed an interest, and I was able to convince them to invest in a joint operation."

"Fascinating," I lied. Thank heavens Mayor Tate chose that moment to indicate we should proceed to the dining room, saving me from any further talk of business.

I soon found myself seated at the long table between Miss Norton and Miss Tate. Mayor Tate sat at one end of the table, with Christine to her right. "I assume you're active in the matter of women's suffrage?" Mayor Tate asked once the parson had droned his way through a lengthy prayer for grace.

Christine's eyes lit up. "Naturally! I must say, I was quite impressed to discover Fallow has a female mayor. The men of your town must be uncommonly sensible."

Mr. Tate and Iskander exchanged a look.

"I am the seventeenth woman to hold such a position in Kansas," Mayor Tate replied modestly. "But it isn't due just to the men—women can vote in municipal elections in our fair state."

"Kansas is far ahead of Massachusetts in such matters, then," Christine said with a scowl. "My own work has left me little time to become involved in suffrage, I fear."

"Perhaps you could speak to women's groups, and show them what we might achieve?" Mayor Tate suggested.

The young ladies seemed uninterested in political matters. "Do you have a large practice in Widdershins, Dr. Whyborne?" Miss Norton asked.

It took a moment for me to realize what she meant. "Oh! No. I'm not that sort of doctor. I work at the museum."

"How fascinating," said Miss Tate. "Oh dear, your wine is getting low—please let me refresh it for you."

Miss Norton shot her friend a glare across me. "Do try the potatoes," she said, adding some to my plate without asking. "I cooked them myself."

"Our cook was considered one of the best in Virginia, before Mother lured him here," Miss Tate said smugly.

Miss Norton's smile grew more and more fixed. "I find a woman should know how things ought to be done first hand. Only then can she judge whether the work of another meets her standards."

"How interesting. I have never found it necessary to know how to plow a field in order to judge whether the resulting meal in front of me is any good."

Miss Norton's face flushed an angry red; apparently the remark carried the weight of some history between them. I shrank back in my chair as far as possible, but neither woman seemed to notice my attempt at a retreat.

"I'm certain a man of Dr. Whyborne's stature would prefer a wife who understands the nature of hard work, so as to provide a suitable home," Miss Norton grated out. "Rather than one who would laze about and see only to her own comforts."

"Mr. Tate," I said loudly. "What were you telling me earlier about grain elevators?"

Tate blinked at me in surprise. "Er…that Loyal Grain provided the funds, and I oversee their operation?"

Clearly he thought me a lunatic. I didn't care. "Fascinating. Please tell me more. Spare no details of their workings, I beg you."

CHAPTER 15

Griffin

THE LANTERN WENT flying, leaving us with only the light from the windows. My elbow struck the ground painfully hard, followed by my chin.

A heavy weight came down on my back, and a moldy stench enveloped me. Fingers scrabbled at my throat, and I strove to buck my assailant off before he could throttle me.

"You'll pay for what you've done," he snarled in my ear. His breath reeked like something rotting in a root cellar.

"Get off him!" Lawrence shouted, and grabbed the man's arm.

My assailant ignored him, fingers continuing to tighten. Black spots showed in my vision, and my hands scrabbled in the dust.

Hooking a handful of loose dirt, I squeezed my eyes shut and threw it over my shoulder and into my attacker's face.

He reared back, clawing at his eyes. At the same moment, Lawrence struck him with the stock of the shotgun. My assailant grunted—then fell away from me at a second blow.

I rolled to my feet, revolver at the ready. The man crouched in the full light of the window—and revulsion brought bile to my throat. The familiar grayish hyphae crawled over his face, like the spread of some fungal growth.

"It's Bottomless Joe!" Lawrence exclaimed in recognition.

My finger hesitated on the trigger.

The man lunged at me, seeming not to care for safety any more than Odell or Evers had. Lawrence brought the stock of his shotgun down hard, and Joe collapsed into the dirt, unmoving.

When it became apparent he was unconscious, I lowered my gun. "You know him?" I asked.

I couldn't see Lawrence's expression in the dimness. "Yeah. Bottomless Joe. They call him that because of how much he could drink. But the booze drove him crazy. He's supposed to be locked up at the poor farm. I guess he got out."

The poor farm. Where Odell had been. Where the crops flourished thanks to the new wells.

"You all right?" Lawrence asked me.

I took a deep, shaky breath. "I'm fine," I said, though what I really wanted to do was strip off my things and bathe. God, how he *smelled*.

"Joe must be the prowler," Lawrence said. "Let's get some rope from the barn—we'll tie him up, and take him back to Mrs. Creigh first thing tomorrow."

"Mrs. Creigh?" I asked.

"The superintendent of the poor farm."

"Really?" I murmured. "This might seem like an odd question, but…did Mrs. Creigh recently take over its management, by any chance?"

Lawrence gave me a puzzled look. "How did you know? She came around the beginning of August, if I remember right. Old Mr. Kendrick died of heart failure, and she was his replacement."

"Heart failure," I said. "Of course."

Lawrence's gaze narrowed. "Griffin…is there something you ain't telling me? You said you're a private detective, and I don't mean to intrude where it's none of my business, but are you here looking into more than just some old artifact?"

"I can't really say," I said, with a little nod meant to confirm his assumption.

"Ah." He tapped his nose with a finger. "I get it. I won't say nothing to anyone."

"I appreciate your discretion," I said, relieved I wouldn't have to make up some fable on the spot. "You keep an eye on our friend here, and I'll retrieve the rope."

I was just returning with the rope, when I heard Lawrence shout. "Wait! Stop!"

I broke into a run. Lawrence stood in the yard in front of the house, staring into the darkness. "Gol darn it," he said. "He came to all the sudden. I showed him the gun, told him not to run, but he did anyway."

And of course Lawrence wasn't the sort to shoot an unarmed man, let alone a lunatic not responsible for his actions. "It isn't your fault," I said.

Lawrence cast a final glance in the direction Bottomless Joe had vanished. "I don't think Joe will be back tonight…but just in case, why don't you come in the house and wait until your friends get back. I'd feel better if I knew you weren't out here alone in the barn."

"As would I," I said, and followed him into the house.

CHAPTER 16

Whyborne

BY THE TIME dinner ended, I knew more of grain elevators than I'd ever wished. The ladies drifted away, Christine and Mayor Tate in deep discussion concerning the rights of women, both in the United States and abroad. Miss Norton and Miss Tate followed them, shooting furious looks at one another as they did so.

The rest of us stepped onto the porch for brandy and cigars. I declined a cigar—the things smelled like burning socks in my opinion, although most men seemed to enjoy them. The air held a slight chill, and I was glad for my coat.

"Dr. Whyborne, might I have a private word with you?" Mr. Tate asked.

Dear lord, he didn't mean to inquire as to my intentions toward his daughter, did he? I could hardly refuse his request, so I followed him to a more secluded end of the wrap-around porch, away from the light spilling from the open doors.

"What can I do for you, Mr. Tate?" I asked.

Tate looked deeply uncomfortable. He turned to stare out at the horizon. Searching for any signs of a distant prairie fire, as Griffin had last night? "The matter is…well, it's a bit awkward," he said apologetically. "Normally I would never repeat any sort of gossip, but at the same time I wouldn't feel right if I didn't warn you."

"Warn me?" I asked blankly.

"Yes." He took a fortifying sip of brandy. "About one of your traveling companions. Griffin Flaherty."

Dinner transformed into a leaden lump in my belly. "What about him, sir?" I asked, letting an edge show in my voice.

"I don't know what he's told you," Tate said, "but the reason he moved away from Fallow was less than savory. There was a scandal."

Damn Tate, and the Kerrs along with him. "Mr. Flaherty consented to return to Fallow to assist with an archaeological survey on his mother's farm." The brandy snifter grew colder under my fingers, frost spreading from my touch. The shadows hid it from Tate, but at the moment, I wasn't sure I even cared.

Tate looked wretchedly uncomfortable. "I wouldn't speak of such things ordinarily," he assured me. "But he was…well. To put it plainly, he was caught committing unnatural acts that would outrage the sensibility of any decent man."

Words burned on my tongue, and the scars on my arm ached. How dare he speak of my husband so? How dare he spread such tales, surely knowing the danger it would put Griffin in, were I the ignorant employer Tate assumed me to be?

I hated him. I hated them all.

"I am not in the habit of listening to gossip and innuendo, sir," I said, and the air grew colder with every word that left my lips. "Especially not when spoken behind a man's back."

Mr. Tate stepped away from me, and I caught a flicker of fear in his eyes. Good. Let him fear me. "Dr. Whyborne, I assure you, I worry only for your reputation!"

"And you believe it can only be protected by smearing that of another man?" My face felt like a rigid mask, which might crack at any moment and expose the rage seething within. "I will overlook this lapse, Mr. Tate, because I am a guest in your home. But do not think to whisper slander in my ears again."

"Y-Yes. Forgive me," he said, shrinking back. "I never meant offense."

"You have given it nonetheless." I put my snifter down on the railing. The brandy within had frozen solid. "I believe it time for us to return to our lodgings. Good night to you, sir."

~ * ~

I fumed in silence all the way back to the Reynolds' farm. I'd managed to remain civil until the ladies rejoined us, although the demands of politeness had sorely tried what little patience I had left. When we'd announced our departure, Miss Norton brought out a basket for me.

"A pumpkin pie, as promised. You can return the basket whenever you'd like," she said, giving me a wide smile.

"Did you enjoy your conversation with Mayor Tate, dearest?" Iskander asked when we were well away.

"Oh indeed. We spoke of universal suffrage. Of course, the women's movement is dreadfully tied up with temperance." Christine sighed. "I don't see why I have to give up whiskey in order to gain the vote."

"Very unfair," Iskander agreed.

"However, I didn't allow myself to become entirely distracted by our debate," she went on. "I asked her if she knew a Mr. Delancey."

A bold move—but one I should have expected. "Did she?"

"Quite well," she said, flicking the reins. "I couldn't help but overhear some of your dinner conversation, Whyborne. Mr. Delancey was the man who put her husband in touch with Loyal Grain, made introductions, and generally oversaw the company's operation in Fallow. At least until he was suddenly called back east on business."

Blast. "Do you think the Tates have any connection with the cult?" Of course, we weren't even entirely certain what Delancey's connection had been. If he'd worked with them, or pretended to, or simply been an unknowing pawn who'd realized their intentions too late.

"You spoke alone to Mr. Tate," Iskander said to me. "Did you receive any hint he might be with the Fideles?"

"No." I ground my teeth together. "He wished to warn me that my association with Griffin would do my reputation no good." The slow burning anger threatened to flare up again. "I wanted to strike him. No—I wanted to curse him, in the most literal way possible."

Christine switched to Arabic and described Mr. Tate's ancestry, sexual habits, and general cleanliness in increasingly derogatory terms. "He's a vile excuse of a man," Iskander agreed, once Christine had run out of steam.

Iskander was right…and yet, more people would hold Mr. Tate entirely justified, and Griffin and I entirely in the wrong.

The moonlight showed us the darkened buildings of the Reynolds farm. We climbed down from the wagon, and I opened the barn doors while Iskander and Christine unhitched the mules. There was no sign of Griffin. Perhaps he'd decided to sleep in the house rather than the loft with me? I couldn't help but feel disappointment as I seated myself on a convenient hay bale and removed the pie from the basket.

"As for myself, I spoke to Parson Norton," Iskander said as he led the mules into their stall. They both put down their heads and began to investigate their feed immediately. "I inquired as to any local legends, which might give us some clue as to what we're facing."

Christine pulled up a milking stool and sat down. "Share the pie around, Whyborne," she said. "Did the parson have anything interesting to say, Kander?"

"Just the same stories about the fallow place Griffin already told us." Iskander took out one of his knives and sliced the pie, using his handkerchief in place of a plate. I passed him my handkerchief, and Christine did the same. "Here," he said, handing me a slice. "We might not be able to correct all the injustices of the world tonight, but we can enjoy a dessert made by the award-winning pie maker of the county."

"Who would knife her best friend in the back for a chance at Whyborne," Christine added with a grin.

"It isn't funny, Christine," I said. "I thought I might have to fake my own death to escape them."

"Now that *would* have livened up the evening." She took the second slice from Iskander. "You should have pretended illness and vomited on Mr. Tate."

"If I encounter the man again, I may do it anyway," I muttered. We had no forks, so I lifted the slice to my lips—

"Whyborne! No!" Griffin shouted from the door.

~ * ~

Before I could react, Griffin struck the pie from my hand, sending it flying into the dirt. "Dear God! Has anyone eaten any?"

His eyes were wide and wild, his skin so pale his freckles stood out like drops of blood. "No," Christine said, and cast a worried glance at Iskander. He shook his head.

"Thank Christ." Griffin leaned heavily against my shoulder and passed a hand over his face. "The pie…it's corrupted."

I stared at the dessert in horror…but it looked perfectly ordinary to my sight. *"Corrupted?* Like Odell and Marian?"

Griffin nodded. "Seething. It's…not something you wish to see, believe me."

Bile rose in my throat. "I don't understand. How is that even possible? I thought it was something the Fideles, or their pawns, had done to themselves. How can a pie be corrupted?"

"Clearly, we've misunderstood what the corruption is," Christine said. She took the rest of the pie and set it on the ground, well away from the hay bales. Taking Griffin's lantern from him, she shut it off, then splashed oil over the pie. Iskander used the mucking shovel to scoop up the piece Griffin had struck from my hand. Once he stepped back, I lit the oil with a word.

Only when the pie was reduced to charred fragments did Griffin seem to relax. "That appears to have destroyed it. There's no trace remaining in my shadowsight."

"Bloody hell." Iskander sank down onto the hay bale and put his head in his hands. "Was Miss Norton trying to poison us?"

"Christine's right. We've misunderstood." My heart beat almost painfully hard. "What if this is how the corruption is spread? Like a disease?" I looked up, saw expressions of horror on my companion's faces. "What if Odell, Evers, and Marian haven't sided with the Fideles in whatever awful scheme the cult has concocted? What if they're unwilling—unknowing—victims?"

Just as my friends were of the maelstrom's manipulation.

"If you're right, Miss Norton might be corrupted as well," Iskander said. "Or she might be a sorceress, or the apprentice of one. She made the pie with a corrupted pumpkin, intending Whyborne should eat it and become infected as well."

Christine looked uncertain. "But to what possible end?"

The pieces snapped into place. "Mind control," I said. "Odell and Evers's behavior, the fact they all keep repeating the same words to Griffin…"

"And we know from last July that the Fideles are more than willing to use mind control to achieve their ends." Christine said with a shudder. She'd been one of Bradley's victims, taken over for a short time in order to isolate her from the rest of us. Iskander put a comforting hand to her arm.

Griffin stared at the cooling ashes in horror. "God. If I hadn't looked out the window and seen you'd returned…"

"I was surprised to find you in the house, instead of waiting in the barn," I admitted.

He sat on the hay bale beside me. "I had an adventure of my own," he said. "Mrs. Reynolds heard a sound outside. When Lawrence and I went to investigate, I was attacked by another corrupted man."

A hiss of worry escaped me. "Are you unhurt?"

"Quite." He patted my hand reassuringly. "Although if Lawrence hadn't been there, I might have fared far worse. I didn't recognize the man, but he repeated the same words to me that all of the other corrupted have. He escaped, but not before Lawrence recognized him as one of the unfortunates from the poor farm."

"Odell was from the poor farm," I said.

Griffin nodded. "There's more. The superintendent, Mrs. Creigh, has only been here a few months. She came when the old superintendent died rather suddenly."

"You think she's one of the Fideles?" I asked. "She killed the old superintendent and took over, while the other members of the cult were drilling?"

"If the corruption is a form of mind control spread through food, they could easily use it against the inhabitants of the poor farm." Griffin's mouth narrowed with suppressed anger. "They already have no one able to look after them, no one to complain if the Fideles transform them into—into minions to serve their dark purposes. Whatever those might be."

Iskander frowned at the ashes of the pie. "But Marian has no connection with the poor farm. Nor does Miss Norton."

"The poor farm is close to the Kerr farm, though," I argued. "Just on the other side of the fallow place. And Miss Norton's father is the local preacher; no doubt his ministry takes him there often."

"She may even have made a special trip to get the pumpkin," Griffin added. "Given it's one of the few places with flourishing crops, thanks to the new wells."

Christine met my gaze, and I knew we were thinking the same thing. "The wells," she said. "And the sphere."

My fingers felt cold as the implication settled on me. "Delancey called it a transferal sphere. And you said something had burned it out from the inside."

"The corruption?" Griffin asked, his eyes going wide.

"Possibly?" I spread my hands apart helplessly. "What if something was released from the sphere ages ago? It lurked beneath the field, poisoning the land—or, more likely, feeding on the life of anything that tried to take root. Perhaps they searched for the sphere merely because it was an indicator of where the main body of the corruption lay, rather than an end unto itself."

"The water is contaminated," Christine said, going pale. "Spreading the corruption through the crops."

"Then why aren't Mrs. Kerr and Vernon corrupted?" Iskander countered.

"Because the house garden is still watered from the old well." Griffin rubbed at his eyes. "Dear God. If it wasn't, would they be infected as well?"

"If Christine is right, their corn harvest will be infected." I felt as though something with a thousand legs walked down my spine. "Oh, curse me for a fool. The elevators and shipping were taken over by *Loyal* Grain."

"Loyal," Griffin said. "As in Faithful. Fideles."

"Yes." I met his gaze, and the metallic taste of fear filled my mouth. "The corn. As soon as the harvest is done with, they mean to ship it."

"To where?" Griffin asked with a frown.

"Widdershins."

CHAPTER 17

Whyborne

I **AWAITED** **GRIFFIN** in the loft while he locked the door behind Iskander and Christine. "Griffin?" I asked when he joined me. "Is something wrong? Other than the obvious, I mean."

The hay crackled softly as he sank down beside me. His green gaze fixed on his hands, folded in his lap. "I can't stop thinking. If I'd been just a minute later…Last July, when Bradley stole your body… looking at you and not *seeing* you…it was horrible. If this corruption had taken you, I don't know what I would have done."

Oh. I reached out and put my hand over his. "Don't torture yourself over what didn't happen."

His fingers remained limp beneath mine, rather than curling to meet my grasp. "Benjamin is dead. Suicide."

I didn't know what to say. Tate's words came back to me—his concern for my reputation, his willingness to spread slander against Griffin. My stomach clenched, and my scars drew hot and tight.

"He was my friend," Griffin went on, his eyes distant. "I wanted him, and he wanted me, and…he's dead because of it."

"It isn't your fault."

"Isn't it? They didn't let him forget. Lawrence said as much." Griffin shook his head wretchedly. "Someone sent him letters, anonymous ones. And the papers kept the scandal alive."

Why had I let Tate speak to me as he had without consequence? I should have bound his tongue with ice, sent him fleeing into the night to wander the plains alone. "It still wasn't your fault."

"We knew we couldn't afford to be caught, and yet we fucked in the barn anyway." Griffin's voice grew harsh. "And I *left*, Whyborne. I thought we were lucky not to end up in jail, so I left him here to face the consequences, while I flitted off and enjoyed my life in Chicago."

"You didn't know," I insisted. "And the two of you did nothing wrong." Mostly, anyway—Benjamin had been engaged to Marian at the time, after all. But if she'd forgiven him, then the matter should have been over and done with. "He didn't deserve what happened to him."

Griffin swallowed audibly. "I was glad he stayed behind. I thought, maybe, without him…oh God."

I caught him up in my arms, held him tight. He tucked his face against my shoulder. "I can't lose you, Ival," he whispered. "I can't."

"Shh." I kissed his hair. "We haven't lost one another yet."

Yet. So much for my foolish hope that he'd find a home here, once I told him the awful truth. *Could* I tell him, when he already felt so abandoned, so adrift? But if I didn't, he'd return to Widdershins with me. He'd never escape the horror and pain he'd spoken of to the Mother of Shadows.

It wasn't a problem I could solve tonight. So I only held him, and wished there was some way to change things. Or, failing that, some way to make those who'd tormented Benjamin pay for what they'd done.

~ * ~

The ear-splitting caterwaul of the rooster awoke me the next morning.

I'd slept poorly yet again. Even after I fell asleep, curled deep in the hay at Griffin's side, my dreams had waked me several times. I couldn't recall the dreams themselves, but they'd left me with the haunting sensation of a half-glimpsed pattern to…something.

Now Griffin shook my shoulder. "Time to wake up, Ival. Diablo is saying he misses you."

"More likely he's summoning the legions of hell to do his bidding on the earth," I muttered.

By the time I finished washing up, Griffin and Lawrence were already at work in the barn. Griffin had taken the milking stool and tin pail, and gone to the stalls holding the cows. "Care to try?" he asked me.

I eyed the first cow's swollen udder uncertainly. At least she seemed unlikely to attempt to murder me, but I wasn't entirely sure I was up to touching that part of her. Would it feel rubbery, or…?

"Of course, you could feed the chickens again," Griffin said with a grin. Lawrence tried to cover a laugh with a cough, rather unsuccessfully.

I put my shoulders back. "Very well," I declared. "I shall."

Lawrence nodded. "That's the spirit. Don't let the chickens win."

I left them to their puerile snickering and filled the feed bucket. Griffin thought to have a laugh at my expense, but I'd show him. Yesterday, I'd simply been taken by surprise. Today, Diablo would learn I wasn't about to be bullied by a rooster.

~ * ~

I fled into the front yard, Diablo in full pursuit. Somehow, he managed to gain enough altitude to strike me about the head with his wings. I windmilled my arms, trying to protect myself from his merciless assault.

"Hit him with the bucket!" Simon shouted from the porch.

I waved the bucket wildly. It swung unexpectedly on its handle and struck me on the side of the head.

"Go away!" I shouted. "Get back, you infernal creature!"

My foot caught on a stone protruding from the desiccated ground, and I sprawled into the lane. I flung up my arms, certain the Satanic fowl would latch onto my head.

When no attack came, I cautiously lowered my arms again. Apparently satisfied with my humiliation, Diablo strutted back the way we'd come, no doubt returning to his hens with a tale of his heroic battle.

There came a derisive snort from close by. In my agitated state, I hadn't noticed the rider sitting in the lane in front of the house. I blinked as the horse drew closer, then raised my gaze from its legs and found Vernon smirking down at me.

I scrambled to my feet. "What are you doing here?"

His gaze went to the dusty knees of my trousers. "You ain't nothing to worry about," he said. "Don't know why anyone would bother to get worked up about you."

I blinked. "What? Who...?"

But the answer seemed obvious. Nella had surely had any number of harsh things to say about me. And Vernon doubtless knew the accusations James had made, that I was a devil who practiced the blackest of magics.

"As for what I'm doing here, I wanted to make sure my cousin saw this," he said, tossing a rolled up newspaper at me. I tried to catch it and missed.

He turned his horse and cantered away. I scooped up the newspaper from the dust and shook it out.

The *Fallow Tribune* was a slim volume, no more than four pages, and most of that taken up with advertising. The largest headline was dedicated to the *Columbia's* successful defense of the America's Cup. Beneath it ran a notice of a meeting for the local Poultry Association. But the article Vernon had no doubt meant us to see occupied a prominent space near the bottom of the front page.

LUNATIC RETURNS
Disturbs Peace at Kerr Farm

Yesterday a known lunatic made an unexpected appearance, after an absence of some years. The initial departure of Griffin Flaherty is a matter of local memory. If the wholesome air of Fallow did not prevent him from moral insanity, Chicago only compounded his mental instability. This paper has learned that his secretive return to Fallow four years ago was not due to illness, as had been put around at the time, but instead came upon his release from an Illinois lunatic asylum.

We have spoken to his family and can say whatever cure the doctors attempted does not seem to have taken hold. Moreover, Mr. Flaherty has returned with very curious traveling companions. Among them are Mr. and Mrs. Iskander Barnett: Mr. Barnett is an Arab and his wife is a white woman. They are staying on the Reynolds farm.

Also with them is a man of some breeding, who
ought to know better. We wonder if his father is aware
of the company he keeps?

"Whyborne?" Griffin called from behind me. "Was that Vernon I
saw riding away?"

I desperately wanted to hide the newspaper from him. To protect
him from yet more pain. But even if he hadn't already seen the paper
in my hand, I owed him the truth.

"Yes," I said heavily. "Fetch Christine and Iskander from the
house, if you would. They'll want to see this as well."

CHAPTER 18

Griffin

"I'M GOING STRAIGHT to the farm and giving Vernon a good thrashing," Christine snarled, crushing the newspaper in her hands as though imagining it to be Vernon's neck. "And once I'm done with him, the editor of this rag will be next."

"Agreed," Whyborne said. Someone who didn't know him would have mistaken his impassive expression for calm. But the very impassivity of it, save for the tightness at the corners of his mouth and the flare of his nostrils, betrayed him to be in a high fury.

"No," I said. The four of us gathered near the wagon, while the Reynolds went inside for breakfast. Whatever appetite I'd had was gone now, replaced by a sick, sinking feeling.

It was one thing for Vernon to throw me out of the home I'd grown up in. Certainly it hadn't made me happy, but I could do nothing about it if Ma made no move to stop him.

But this? To contact some friend on the newspaper—probably the editor Mr. Carson—and use it to smear not only my reputation, but to insult my friends as well?

My old family, attacking my new one. And all because of me.

"Why the devil not?" Christine demanded. "They both deserve a horse-whipping."

"Because it will do us no good if you and Whyborne are in jail," Iskander pointed out. His dark eyes flashed with anger, but he held up a calming hand. "Please try to remember we have far bigger worries."

"I don't care," Whyborne said unexpectedly.

I put a hand to his arm, felt him trembling with suppressed anger. "Ival?"

"To hell with this town." His nostrils flared. "The Fideles can have it. They deserve one another."

I tightened my grip on him. "You don't mean that."

"Don't I?"

"Marian is corrupted. My *mother* is in danger." I shook my head angrily. "And if that isn't enough, Widdershins is in danger as well."

He shut his eyes and took a deep breath. Then let it out with a sigh. "You're right," he said unhappily. "I have a responsibility. But perhaps it would be best if the rest of you left."

"What nonsense are you blathering now?" Deprived of another outlet, Christine turned her anger on him instead.

"I'll remain here and deal with the Fideles." He swallowed. "And if Widdershins is in danger, it would be best none of you return there. I suggest Boston."

What on earth had gotten into him? Before I could think of any response, Christine said, "Of all the idiotic things I've heard you say, Whyborne, this is the topper."

He drew himself up to his full height. "I'm trying to keep you safe!"

Christine glared up at him, her hands on her hips. "Don't be absurd. Miss Norton already tried to feed you corrupted pie. Without Griffin, how are you to know what's safe to eat? Who isn't—or is—a sorcerer?"

"I'll eat from cans," Whyborne said stubbornly. "And I'll just assume everyone is out to do me in."

"Oh, yes, that will work splendidly." Christine rolled her eyes.

I put a hand to his elbow before he could continue the argument. "Ival, please, you're being irrational. How could you possibly think any of us would leave you to save our own skins? For God's sake, I ventured into an underground city full of umbrae for you in Alaska."

"And I'm certainly not giving up my career to move to Boston of all places," Christine exclaimed. "Good gad, man, the nonsense you spout."

"I...yes." He deflated. "You're right. I just wish..."

"Us to be safe. I know." I glanced at the house. "Now, if you're finished being dramatic, we need to determine our next move."

"The poor farm seems to be the epicenter of the corruption," Iskander said quickly.

I nodded. "Agreed. I'd like to have the opportunity to look around. Unfortunately, I don't see any way to accomplish that during the daylight without being spotted by the residents, if not the Fideles."

"Some of whom might be inclined to attack you, if they're corrupted," Iskander agreed.

Whyborne leaned against the wagon, frowning into space. "I still don't understand why the corrupted seem determined to hurt Griffin. Except for Marian. But whatever motive she might have had, even she spoke the same words to him as the others."

"If the corruption is a form of mind control, as seems likely, perhaps the cultist who is commanding them has a particular grudge against Griffin?" Iskander suggested.

Christine tapped at her chin thoughtfully with a finger. "Likely either Mr. Tate or Mrs. Creigh is controlling them," she said. "Assuming Tate isn't just a pawn, unaware of with whom he's allied. Does Creigh's name sound familiar, Griffin?"

"No." I ran my hand back through my hair, resisting the urge to tug at it in frustration. "But she might use an alias. Possibly I crossed her in my Pinkerton days, and she was delighted to find she had the opportunity for revenge."

"Mrs. Creigh," Christine mused. "Is there a Mr. Creigh?"

"Not that Lawrence mentioned."

"Hmm. Perhaps you widowed her last July in our fight against the cultists, and she wants revenge."

Iskander frowned. "In the confusion of the battle, I'm hard pressed to imagine how anyone would know exactly who killed whom. Unless she was literally standing right there."

"I suppose," she agreed.

"It doesn't matter," I said. "We'll wait until sundown and visit the poor farm." I lowered my voice. "Lawrence is under the impression I'm here on detective business, so our sneaking out at night won't seem suspicious to him."

"Good thinking," Whyborne said. I didn't have the heart to tell him it hadn't been my idea. "Griffin, I'd like you to take a close look at the corn fields. Just to confirm they're corrupted. I don't want to take any drastic action like destroying the grain elevators if we don't know for certain."

Christine arched a brow. "Is that your plan? I don't suppose you have dynamite lying around?"

"I don't need dynamite," he snapped irritably. "Really, Christine."

"Then we'll sneak in through the unharvested corn," I decided, heading off another argument. "It will offer some cover to our approach to the poor farm."

"Agreed," Whyborne said. "And what shall we do until tonight?"

I clapped him on the shoulder. "Chores, of course. How do you feel about mucking out stalls?"

~ * ~

It was well after midnight when we drew the wagon to a halt a quarter mile or so away from the poor farm's boundary. The farm lay a short distance to the north and east of Ma's farm. I'd visited the place twice in my youth: once when Pa and some of our hired hands apprehended an escaped lunatic, and once to take donated blankets from the church.

The poor farm housed the folk of the county who could no longer support themselves, or whose family couldn't provide for them. Orphans, the elderly, those crippled by accident or disease, those suffering from tuberculosis, even the mad whose cases weren't desperate enough for them to be sent to the state hospital in Topeka: all were taken in by the poor farm. Those who could work the land did so, while the rest were at least ensured a roof over their head and three meals a day.

The mules balked sharply, tossing their heads. "Whoa," I soothed. "What's spooked you?"

"Just like yesterday," Christine said from where she sat on the driver's seat beside me.

"Yesterday?"

Whyborne sat in the back of the wagon. Now he got to his knees and peered out between Christine and me. "After we left you in front of your mother's house, the mules balked. We thought perhaps they smelled a predator?"

"Perhaps." Or perhaps I wasn't the only one who could sense the presence of the corruption.

I secured the mules to a fence post, and Whyborne took the lantern from the wagon. I would have preferred to have gone without a light, but there was no moon, and the blaze of the stars wouldn't be enough for our task. Christine took her rifle from the back of the wagon and tossed my sword cane to me. My revolver I already carried in my pocket.

"Ready?" I asked.

Iskander patted his coat, which concealed his knives. "Lead on."

As we approached the corn, my steps slowed. Every stalk glowed faintly in my shadowsight, but the light was threaded through with veins of darkness. "It's all corrupted," I said. "Every plant."

Iskander winced. "We'd guessed as much, but confirmation is hardly pleasant."

Whyborne led the way to the irrigation ditch. The water glowed with an unnatural light, just like the corn. I crouched beside the ditch, not daring to touch the water, and inspected it as carefully as I could. It looked muddy, filled with some kind of black sediment, whose tiny particles remained suspended, rather than settling to the bottom.

When I described what I saw, Whyborne shuddered. "Like spores," he said.

The blood drained from my skin, and I hastily stood up and stepped back a pace. "Exactly like spores."

"Well, this certainly grows more and more horrifying," Iskander muttered. "Forgive me, Griffin, but I can't say your hometown has proven a pleasant locale to visit."

"I see why it's dying," Christine observed. "The town boosters don't have much to work with. Fallow: come for the vicious gossip and slanderous newspapers; stay for the magical water laden with infectious spores."

"It makes Widdershins seem almost pleasant in comparison," I replied lightly.

Whyborne flinched, though, as if I'd slapped him. "We should hurry, before anyone sees us," he said, and started off without waiting.

As we moved deeper into the field, the light of the arcane line grew brighter and brighter in my vision. Though it was nothing compared to the vortex in Widdershins. *That* was a sight indeed: rivers of glowing fire, all converging on a single point. If it had been visible to the ordinary eye, it would be considered a landmark of great beauty. The sort of place where artists would come to paint, and tourists to gawk.

But I was the only one who could see it. Just as I was the only one who had glimpsed what lived in Ival's skin, in those moments when it was released from the bonds of the flesh. The thought made me feel strangely warm.

The breeze grew stronger, the leaves of the corn rattling against each other. We were deep in the corn now, perhaps halfway to our goal. Whyborne came to an abrupt halt, a frown on his face. "Does anyone feel any actual wind?"

We all froze instantly. The corn continued to hiss, as if in a strong gust, but he was right. There was no breath of air against my skin to accompany it.

A low moan sounded off to the right.

"What was that?" Whyborne whispered hoarsely. "It sounded like what I heard the other day, before Vernon found me."

There came another moan, but this one was from the left.

I drew out my revolver. "Hurry," I said. "We need to get out of the field."

Whyborne nodded. "Agreed," he said, and took a step forward.

A corrupted figure surged up from the ground at his feet.

CHAPTER 19

Whyborne

AN INVOLUNTARY SHOUT escaped me as a figure rose up right in front of me. Then I got a good look at it in the light of my lantern, and barely bit back a second cry.

It was human, or had been once. But its utterly hairless skin had turned a dark gray, slick and wet as something rotting beneath the ground. Bulging veins crawled over its body and face, distended and throbbing with corruption.

It had been lying there, silent in the corn, until I nearly trod on it.

It was silent no more. Its mouth gaped open in a moan, revealing teeth furred in black mold. A revolting smell burst forth, a mixture of rot and mildew that flooded my mouth with bile. It lifted hands whose nail-less fingers were swollen and slick—and lunged at me.

"Ival! Get down!" Griffin shouted.

I ducked. The crack of his revolver rang out, and the corrupted thing jerked, then collapsed, half its head missing.

I scrambled back, even as the corn began to thrash around us, as if in the midst of a storm. Other moans sounded, closer now—the things must have been lying in wait, their presence concealed even to Griffin's sight by the glare of the arcane line and the glow of the corn itself.

"Run!" Griffin shouted, and grabbed me by the arm. One of the corrupted lunged from the adjoining row, its slimy hands barely missing my throat as Griffin hauled me back.

Then we were running, the corn rippling and rolling around us in great waves. I cast a glance back, saw more of the corrupted stagger from the rows. What spell could I use against them? Fire was no good; if I burned down the field, we'd likely end up roasted along with it. Possibly half the county as well, if it turned into a prairie fire. Wind? But on the open plains, there was nothing to funnel its force. Perhaps lightning, if we could stop running for a minute—but that, too, risked fire if there was a spark.

The corrupted came faster now, breaking into a slow run from their initial shamble.

A moaning figure stepped out in front of us. Christine didn't hesitate; the crack of her rifle shattered the air. Her aim was true; half its head burst apart in a spray of gray nastiness.

A moan sounded right behind me. I spun—and hands closed around my throat.

The touch of the corrupted's rubbery skin filled me with instinctive revulsion. I thrashed, clutching at its soft flesh, which gave sickeningly beneath my nails.

Iskander's knives flashed down, severing one of the corrupted's arms. The knife passed through easily, as though there was no bone left inside, nothing but a sort of spongey sameness, like slicing through the cap of a mushroom. A second flash, and the other arm was severed.

Both continued to clutch at my neck.

I cried out in disgust, but was able to rip them away. The corrupted didn't seem to have noticed their loss, merely staggered toward me again.

I laid frost on its skin. The places my spell touched instantly turned black and flaked off, but it wasn't enough to do more than slow the creature down.

"Come on, Whyborne!" Griffin exclaimed. "We have to outrun them!"

We tore through the corn, cutting across rows as we struggled to get out of the field. Another corrupted emerged to one side, and

Iskander sliced off its head with a single blow, the soft flesh giving way as human ligament and bone never would. Griffin shot another in the chest; it staggered but didn't stop until he ran his sword cane through its eye.

We burst out of the field and into the open air.

A cluster of buildings stood not far away: a large house where the poor farm's inmates no doubt lived, a quarantine building for those with tuberculosis or other disease, equipment sheds, barns, and chicken coops. Christine paused, bracing herself to fire again, and the rest of us fell in beside her.

The rustling amidst the corn died away. I glimpsed dark figures moving between the rows, slowly withdrawing, as if they didn't wish to pass the boundaries of the field. Because something tied them to the place, or because they'd been set only to guard the corn from trespassers?

"Bloody hell," Iskander said shakily. "What *are* they?"

"The final stage of the infection?" I suggested. "They seemed more fungal than animal."

"God." Griffin shook his head. "We have to find a cure. If this is what awaits Marian…whatever she might think of me, she's family."

"Well, we've made it this far," Christine said, slinging her rifle over her shoulder again. "We ought to have a look around."

Keeping a wary eye on the main house, we made our way amidst the cluster of buildings. The coops stood open and empty, and there were no signs of cats or dogs, or even tracks of rabbits near the flourishing gardens.

"It's all corrupted," Griffin whispered with a nod at the gardens. "The pumpkins, greens—everything. Just like the corn."

"So where do we look?" I asked. "Do we dare try to sneak into the main house?"

"What's that?" Iskander asked. The building he pointed to stood well away from the main house, not far from the section of the field that had already been harvested. It was small, its only windows were set too high to look in or out of.

"The jail, I expect," Griffin murmured.

"Jail?"

"For the inmates who are deranged," he clarified. "Those who are a danger to others, and can't be kept in the main house where they might hurt someone else."

Christine started for the jail. "Let's see who—or what—Mrs. Creigh might be keeping in there."

When we reached the building, she tried the door. "Locked," she confirmed in a low voice. "Griffin, did you think to bring your housebreaking tools?"

He nodded. "Of course. Whyborne, bring the lantern closer."

I did so. He knelt in front of the door and took out the leather wallet containing his lock picks. In the space of a few minutes, there came a click, and he rose to his feet. "There." He tucked the wallet back into his vest. "Stand ready."

The door swung open with a squeal of hinges, and I shone the light inside.

~ * ~

The smell rolled over me like a fetid wave: unwashed bodies, human waste, and above all the earthy stench of mildew, as if the jail were a root cellar or a cave rather than an aboveground building.

I pulled out my handkerchief and clapped it over my mouth. Christine did the same; Iskander coughed heavily into his sleeve. "Phagh!" he exclaimed. "What a reek."

Griffin's face had turned the color of cottage cheese. His lips parted, and I didn't know if he meant to vomit or cry out.

The interior was divided into four small cells, three of them occupied. The unfortunates within had no bedding, nothing at all to keep their naked skin from the hardness of the concrete floor they lay on. Their flesh had taken on a horrible, grayish hue, their scalps visible where their hair had begun to fall out in clumps. Worst of all, patches of a sort of slick, blackish mold had erupted across their skin, as thought something inside them pushed its way to the surface.

"This is where Creigh is making the…the sort of corrupted we met in the field." The fine hairs stood up on the back of my neck. Was there some spell, some process, which compelled the infection to alter its host this profoundly? Odell certainly hadn't looked anything like this—and if he had begun to in time, his usefulness would surely have come to an end very quickly.

As would mine, if I'd eaten the pie.

"This can't be a final stage," I whispered. "It's deliberate."

The nearest corrupted inmate opened his eyes.

They were no longer human, the capillaries replaced by gray-black hyphae, the corneas dead and lifeless. As one, the trapped souls around us rose to their feet. The foul stench billowed out from them, and bile clawed at the back of my throat. The four of us instinctively crowded together, back to back, and I found myself desperately glad for the bars separating us from the infected.

"Let's go," Griffin said tightly, grabbing my hand. "We need to get out of here, before they raise an alarm."

I let him pull me away from the jail and into the clean night air. "What do we do?" Christine asked. "We can't just—just *leave* them!"

"It's too late for them," Griffin said. "There was almost nothing human left in my shadowsight."

"But we——" She fell silent.

We were no longer alone.

A large group of men and women dressed in their nightclothes shuffled from the house toward us. I didn't need to hear Griffin's gasp to guess that every one of them was surely corrupted.

At their head walked a woman who exuded power even though she wore a dressing gown. Unbound blond hair trailed down her back, and her dark eyes flashed in the light of our lantern. Around her throat, she wore a necklace set with a black jewel threaded through with purple veins.

"Christine, put down your rifle," Griffin ordered. "She's a sorceress."

Christine swore and let the rifle fall to the ground. Griffin unsheathed his sword cane and held it out before him.

"Well, well," the woman said. "If it isn't Dr. Whyborne. You should have let me know you intended to visit—I might have worn something a bit more suitable."

Her lack of concern sent a chill down my spine. I straightened my shoulders and did my best not to let it show. "Mrs. Creigh, I presume."

She inclined her head in the direction of the jail. "Indeed. I see you found where we hold those in the process of becoming cinereous."

"Cinereous?" I asked. My heart beat knocked against my ribs, and I tried to think of how we might escape.

"I refer to those you encountered in the corn," she replied. "I'll be happy to discuss them with you further. You must have many questions, I'm sure. Lay down your weapons, come with me peacefully, and we'll discuss this like civilized people over drinks and refreshments."

She was obviously hoping I didn't know how the corruption was spread. And without Griffin's shadowsight, I very likely would have had no clue. "Very well," I said. "It's clear you have me at a disadvantage. I accept your invitation."

"Whyb——" Christine started. I trod heavily on her foot.

"Now, now, Christine," I said. "It serves no one to fight."

I started toward Creigh, who arched a brow. "Indeed. I must say, I'm surprised to find you so sensible."

"You should be," I agreed. And with all my strength, I flung the burning lantern into the harvested field.

The dry stubble caught instantly. I fanned the fire with a bit of wind—

It erupted into flame, the desiccated debris of the harvest burning hotter and faster than I'd imagined.

"Run!" I shouted at my companions.

We bolted into the night. "Put out the fire before it reaches the rest of the harvest!" Creigh shouted behind us. Then she began to chant.

The earth turned suddenly soft beneath our feet, slowing our progress. Christine let out a furious oath. I lay down frost, hardening it again.

Then we were past the jail and the empty barn, and out of Creigh's line of sight. "This way!" called Iskander, and I followed the sound of his voice to the lane.

"Whyborne," Griffin panted, "Are you mad? If that starts a prairie fire, it could destroy the entire town!"

"It's the only thing I could think of to distract her," I snapped. Or tried to; lack of breath took much of the force from my words. "I remembered what you said, and hoped she'd divert the corrupted to the task of putting out the fire before it destroys her work."

We reached the road, and I slowed, no longer able to keep pace. Griffin matched his speed to mine. "Truly, it was quick thinking on your part," he said, putting a hand to my elbow. "I don't mean to sound ungrateful."

"Indeed," Christine agreed. In the starlight, I could just make out her rifle as she hefted it. "I was even able to retrieve my rifle in the confusion. Not shoot anyone with it, of course, but well." She patted my arm. "One can't have everything, I suppose."

CHAPTER 20

Whyborne

" **I MUST SAY,** Christine keeping possession of her rifle aside, the evening was a bit of a disaster," Iskander said. We'd retrieved the wagon and returned to the Reynolds farm without any further excitement, the glow of the fire I'd set growing smaller and smaller in the distance.

"We did learn something about the goings on at the poor farm," I suggested weakly.

"And we confirmed that the water is the source of the corruption," Christine added. "But Kander is right. Creigh knows we're onto her now, which means our situation has become even more unpredictable."

"Creigh was commanding the corrupted via the jewel at her throat," Griffin said.

"Really?" I frowned. "The way sorcerers used the Occultum Lapidem in Egypt to control the umbra?" There was a pattern, I thought. I'd dreamed of it last night, hadn't I? Something about the masters' creations, how they were made...

"Exactly," Griffin said. "We should be able to disrupt it with the curse breaking spell."

It was a chance at least. "How are we to get close enough to do so? If we confront Creigh directly, she'll simply call on her corrupted."

Christine narrowed her eyes. "I think you gentlemen are making this far too difficult. Can we lure her away from the poor farm?"

"The community dance is tomorrow," Griffin said thoughtfully. "It would seem strange if she didn't attend. Get-togethers like the dance aren't just a chance to have fun. They're one of the ways people stay in touch with each other, given how far apart the farms are. People eat, talk, re-establish the bonds of community. Under normal circumstances, some of the poor farm residents even come." He sounded as though he was recalling some of those dances, those bonds, himself.

"These blasted plains don't offer many hiding places," Christine said. "I say we wait until after dark, when she's returning, and ambush her. If she has a lantern, I might even be able to use my rifle from a distance, and save us the bother of trying to break the spell."

Iskander looked queasy. "I'm not certain I want to simply assassinate the woman, Christine."

She snorted. "Why not? Because it doesn't seem sporting? Really, Kander, don't be ridiculous. Look at what she's done to those who depended on her at the poor farm! She's taken the most desperate, the most vulnerable, and turned them into monsters. If I have a chance to put a bullet in her skull, I see no reason not to take it."

"Depending on Mr. Tate's involvement, that could leave him still to oppose us," I reminded her. "We don't know if he's a sorcerer or not, but if he is, he could simply step into her place. We must break the spell on the jewel."

"Speaking of Tate," Griffin said, "Whyborne, you need to send a telegram to your father first thing tomorrow morning, followed up by a letter explaining the situation to him. The corn can't be allowed to leave Fallow. And if we fail, and it does leave, it must be quarantined on the boxcars. Tell him to burn them if he must."

I nodded. "Agreed."

"And I…" He hesitated, then sighed. "I have to try to warn Ma."

"Griffin—"

"She's in the same house as Marian, Whyborne." He turned to me, looking desperate. "What will happen if Marian starts to take on the aspect of the cinereous we fought tonight? Or worse—what if Creigh decides to use her against us?"

I didn't want him to go, because I didn't want to see him hurt again. Curse his blasted family, who cared more about who he slept with than the fact he was a good man: strong and kind and so very brave.

"I'll go with you," Iskander offered. "None of us should go anywhere alone now that Mrs. Creigh knows she's discovered. And I feel my presence would be more, er, neutral than others."

Griffin nodded. "Thank you."

"Whyborne and I will head into town as soon as we've had breakfast," Christine decided. She started for the door, then glanced back at me. "Assuming he survives feeding the chickens, of course."

~ * ~

"Damned creature," I muttered, sucking on my finger. The shallow scratch Diablo had left behind to mark his victory still stung even an hour later.

Christine and I rumbled down the road to town in the wagon, having promised the Reynolds to bring back a few things from the general store when we returned. The mules hadn't been pleased at being brought out again so soon after last night, and were currently all but dragging their feet down the road.

"Honestly, Whyborne." Christine gave the reins a little snap, which the mules ignored. "You can command the wind. You can set things on fire with your mind. And yet you allow yourself to be bullied by a five pound bird!"

"It isn't as though I can use my sorcery against it," I replied irritably. "I might injure the awful thing." Assuming Diablo could be hurt by anything short of a stake through the heart, that is.

Christine's snort let me know exactly what she thought of me.

We eventually arrived in town. The place was as dusty and half deserted as it had been our first day in this accursed place. I couldn't wait to leave Fallow behind forever and return to Widdershins.

Going by his remark of last night, Griffin didn't feel the same.

Almost pleasant, those were the words he'd used. In comparison with this abominable town, anyway.

Of course, he'd never hesitated to slander Widdershins in my hearing. Always going on about how in other cities one didn't usually hear muffled chanting after dark, or that cloaked figures would attract suspicion. He'd even complained of the carols our first Christmas together, claiming "Blood on the Altar" wasn't a staple of the holiday season.

And *yes,* there was a bit more grave robbing than could be accounted for, especially in a town with no medical school. Yes, it was inadvisable to go too far into the local forest, if one didn't wish to vanish without a trace. True, it was founded by sorcerers and inhabited by ketoi hybrids, and ghūl hybrids, and enough people went mad we'd needed our own insane asylum before I destroyed it, and…

Oh God. It was a horrible murder town, wasn't it?

Griffin didn't belong in Widdershins. He belonged in Boston, or New York, or San Francisco. But I'd assumed, naively, that he was unaware of it. That he didn't long for the life that should have been.

I had to tell him—tell them all—and soon.

Spirits low, I followed Christine into the general store. While she set about making the Reynolds's purchases, I searched for a new hat, having lost mine somewhere in the field last night. As I did so, a voice exclaimed, "Why Dr. Whyborne, what a pleasant surprise!"

I turned to find Miss Tate behind me, followed by a bevy of young women, which notably lacked Miss Norton.

Had Miss Norton fallen out of favor? Or was she corrupted now, and no longer focused on the business of living her own life, but of carrying out the Fideles' orders?

And what of Miss Tate herself? Did she know of her father's business involvement with the Fideles? Was Mr. Tate an ignorant tool of the cult, or did he work with them in full knowledge?

Manners forced me to respond, even though I would have preferred to take my leave as quickly as possible. "Miss Tate," I said, "the pleasure is mine."

"You haven't been around town much," she said. "I was almost afraid you'd left."

"We'll be here for a few more days," I replied, though I feared the estimate wildly optimistic.

She smiled and stepped closer to me. "Then I'll see you at the dance tonight?"

I didn't dare tell the truth. If she mentioned to her father that I didn't plan on attending, he might suspect we intended to move against Mrs. Creigh.

"You *must* come," she said when I hesitated too long. "It's to celebrate the harvest." Her cupid's bow lips tightened just slightly; surely she knew there wasn't much to celebrate this year. "*Everyone* in Fallow will be there."

"It sounds, er, lovely," I said.

She must have taken the words as encouragement, because she leaned even closer, a smile spreading over her face. "Oh, it will be. Say you'll come and save me from having to sit all alone in the corner?"

I doubted she would lack for male company. "Of course," I lied, and managed something that felt like a smile. "I wouldn't think to miss it."

"Good!" Having secured my agreement, she finally stepped back. "Well, then, I'd best get on to the seamstress's. She's fitting the most lovely gown—straight from New York, you know."

Having been subjected to the highest fashion in the form of interminable parties at Whyborne House, I doubted any dress in Fallow had ever graced Fifth Avenue. When she lived, my elder sister Guinevere wouldn't have been seen in anything not brought all the way from Paris.

"I look forward to seeing it," I lied.

Christine joined me once Miss Tate departed. "Securing your conquest, Whyborne?" she asked me cheerfully.

"Do stop." I selected the least offensive of the hats and placed it on my head. "Let's pay for this and be off to the telegraph office."

The telegraph office occupied a small building at one end of the street. I could hear the hammer clacking merrily as we mounted the steps.

It fell silent as soon as we entered, however. The operator turned around—and an odd look passed over his face, expression flickering so quickly I wasn't certain I'd seen it.

"I need to send a telegram," I said, stepping up to the counter.

"I'm sorry," he said with a regretful shrug. "The telegraph is broken."

Christine scowled. "But you were just using it!"

The operator's gaze remained fixed on me. "No, I wasn't."

It was such a bald-faced lie, I hadn't the slightest idea how to respond. Christine, however, had no such trouble. "Now see here—"

"It's broken, Dr. Whyborne," the operator said to me, as though Christine didn't exist.

Oh. Oh no. I hadn't given my name. And perhaps he might have guessed my identity…but given his odd behavior, I doubted the explanation was so innocent.

He was corrupted. He must be.

"My mistake," I said. "We'll just be on our way."

"Corrupted," Christine agreed as soon as we stepped outside. "Blast. I wish Griffin had come with us after all."

So did I, desperately. "At least we can mail the letter," I said, and made for the post office.

But the man working the counter greeted us with, "How can I help you, Dr. Whyborne?"

We retreated hastily, the letter still in my pocket. "Damn it!" Christine swore once we were back on the street. "How many townspeople have been infected?"

I shook my head. "There's no way of knowing."

"I suppose after Delancey betrayed them, the Fideles want to keep anyone else from warning the outside world of what's happening in Fallow." Christine turned to the train depot. Nearby, the great grain elevators towered up, and a shudder passed through me at the sight of them. "What do you want to bet Creigh has corrupted agents at the depot as well?"

It made sense. "We should go back to the farm and wait for Iskander and Griffin."

"Yes." Christine straightened her shoulders. "If we can't get word to the outside world, and can't leave, we'll simply have to deal with things ourselves. It's all up to us, now."

CHAPTER 21

Griffin

MY FEET FELT heavy by the time I reached the farmhouse, and not just because of the long walk. I didn't know if Ma would even speak to me, or if she'd slam the door in my face. Or what Marian might do—if Creigh would somehow sense my presence and force her to attack me.

Then again, perhaps that would prove my words to Ma, in a way nothing else would.

Vernon and his men would no doubt be in the field, bringing in the tainted crop. I wasn't certain if I was glad or sad that the fire hadn't spread last night. If it had spread, homes might have been lost, people made destitute. But at the same time, if it meant the corrupted corn was destroyed…would that have been worth it?

None of it could ship to the east. Hopefully Loyal Grain had already paid Vernon for the corn delivered to the elevators. Because if not, the entire harvest would be a loss, and all of Vernon's hard work for nothing.

God. I didn't care for Vernon, nor he for me, but I didn't want the farm to fail. What would become of Ma if she lost her home?

Iskander paused in the lane. "Shall I wait out here?"

"Yes. Please."

"Call for help, and I'll come running immediately," he said.

I nodded, grateful for his presence, then made for the house. No one seemed to be about in the outside gardens, which was a relief. I knocked on the door, heard the approach of footsteps, and braced myself.

Ma's eyes widened. "Griffin? What are you doing here?"

Thank heavens, she still wasn't corrupted. And she hadn't yet slammed the door in my face. "I need to talk to you, Ma. Can I come inside?"

She glanced over her shoulder. "You shouldn't be here."

I'd known for years I didn't belong here. In this town. In this house. But hearing it from her made my heart even heavier. "Ruth told me that when Pa came back from Stormhaven, some of the things he said didn't seem possible. That he spoke of sorcery." I took a deep breath. "He wasn't mad. Wrong about the details, but not mad."

She looked at me for a long moment, then stepped back. "You'd best come in."

I followed her inside. She went to the kitchen and took out bread and butter, as if feeding me was an instinct. I sat at the table and waited.

Her back still turned, she said, "Your pa…he weren't in his right mind after that. He claimed he'd been grabbed to use as a hostage, not out of mistaken identity like the police told us. Said *he* was there."

I bit back a flash of anger. "If by 'he' you mean Whyborne, then yes. That's true."

Her hands stilled. "Your pa said he was a devil. That he had some kind of black magic. Threatened James with it. You ain't going to tell me that's true?"

"Whyborne is no devil." How could I explain any of this? "Yes, he was angry at Pa. For forcing me to choose."

She brought buttered bread and tea to the table and set it before me. "When your pa started raving about magic and devils, I thought it was judgment for…well, never you mind." She lowered her voice. "I always thought it was the Walter boy's fault. That he'd tempted you, but then you lived a righteous life after you left Fallow. But here you were, living with *him*. So maybe I was wrong, and the Walter boy wasn't to blame after all."

"No one was to blame." I couldn't argue this with her now, not when I had to convince her Marian was a danger. "None of that matters at the moment. Whatever you think of Whyborne or me, Pa wasn't crazy. He was wrong about Whyborne, but not about the fact that there is sorcery in the world. Magic, which can be turned to purposes both good and evil."

I couldn't read the expression on her face. Shock? Fear? Perhaps even a trace of relief, to think her husband hadn't been unhinged after all? "That's the reason we came to Fallow," I said. "The real reason. There are sorcerers here, and we're going to try to stop them, but I had to warn you. In case we fail. Don't eat anything—*anything*—grown using the water from the new wells. The ones in the fallow place." I swallowed. "And whatever you do, don't be alone with Marian. Lock your bedroom at night."

"It's true," Vernon said from the front door. "You really are crazy."

I surged to my feet, heart thumping. Vernon entered, the floor creaking beneath his boots. Behind me, the back door opened, and I heard multiple steps coming inside.

"Vernon," I said, holding up my hand, "please, just listen."

"Oh, I've heard enough. I think we all have." The grin he offered me was decidedly unpleasant. "Don't blame yourself, Aunt Nella. He was born sick, and there weren't nothing you could do about it."

I backed away from him, heart pounding. "Don't hurt him, Vernon," Ma pleaded. "He's just confused, that's all. Let him go."

"I'm sorry, but I can't do that. He's dangerous to himself, don't you see? Going around talking about magic, slandering my wife—who knows what he might do next." Vernon nodded at the three farm hands who had crowded into the kitchen. "Don't worry, though. The poor farm will keep him safe."

No.

I slammed my shoulder into Vernon's chest. Taken off guard by the move, he staggered back, and I ran out the front door.

I leapt down the porch stairs and into the yard. Feet thudded behind me, but I didn't dare look back. Instead, I drew my revolver, intending to threaten them into letting me go.

"Iskander!" I called. "Run!"

A heavy weight smashed into me, bearing me to the ground. My chin clipped the sunbaked earth, hard enough to send a burst of stars across my vision. Before I could recover, a hand closed over my wrist, pinning it to the ground while the gun was wrestled away.

Then the beating started.

I curled into a ball, shielding my organs and my head as best I could. Fists and feet rained down on me, accompanied by foul curses. It flashed through my mind that I might die here. They might beat me to death in the lane in front of the very house I'd grown up in.

"Stop!" Iskander shouted.

One of the men cried out. "He has a knife!" another yelled.

I tried to roll to my knees while they were distracted, but a flare of agony in my ribs slowed me. Blood ran into my eyes from a cut in my scalp. I dashed it away just in time to see one of them scoop up my revolver and aim it at Iskander.

He froze, eyes going wide. "Put down the knives, camel-fucker," said the man. "Don't think I won't shoot you."

Iskander's knives fell to the dusty ground. "Bind them both," Vernon ordered.

"Stop!" Ma shouted. "Let them go."

"Go back in the house, Aunt Nella," Vernon replied. "This ain't your business no more."

Agony shot through me as the men hauled me to my feet, and I spat out a gobbet of blood. Vernon seized my aching jaw and forced my head back. I half expected him to be smiling in triumph, but instead rage transformed his features. "You ain't nothing," he growled into my face. "Hear me? Nothing but dirt. And you'll pay for what you did."

It was the phrase that had been used so often by the corrupted… but Vernon wasn't corrupted. And yet I couldn't believe it a coincidence.

He let go of me and stepped back, wiping his hands against his trousers, as if my very touch might have contaminated him. "Bring around the cart, boys," he said. "And take them to the poor farm. We'll let Mrs. Creigh take care of things."

CHAPTER 22

Whyborne

"WHERE THE DEVIL are they?" Christine exclaimed, pacing across the barn floor yet again. The late afternoon sunlight spilled in through the open doors, and the sound of clucking chickens drifted on the breeze. I kept a sharp eye out for Diablo, but the fiend failed to put in an appearance. No doubt he was busy eating children or terrorizing cattle.

"I don't know." I sat on the milking stool, picking apart a hunk of bread left over from our lunch with the Reynolds hours ago. My appetite had been poor even then, and the hours of waiting hadn't improved it. "Clearly they were delayed."

"We have to do something," Christine said. "Kander and Griffin should have been back hours ago. Griffin might get distracted by his mother and forget the time, but Kander wouldn't."

"I said they were delayed." I rose to my feet. "Not that the delay was innocent."

Christine swore, but I'd only spoken aloud what we'd both surely been thinking. "Damn it! We should never have let them go without us. Blast Griffin, anyway—why did he feel he had to warn the wretched woman?"

Although I sympathized with Christine's sentiment, I felt compelled to defend my husband. "Because Nella raised him, and he still loves her."

"Bah." Christine scowled. "Well. We need to find them, that's all."

"But where do we look? The Kerr farm? Or were they accosted along the way?" Oh God, what if they were lying in a ditch somewhere? What if the corrupted had ambushed them? What if...?

No. I wouldn't consider the possibility that something fatal had occurred. The very thought was unbearable.

Christine looked to be entertaining similar worries. "I'll fetch my rifle."

I stuffed the bread into my pocket. "Do. We'll go to the Kerr farm first."

"Agreed." Christine said, striding to the door. "I—"

She fell abruptly silent, eyes narrowing. Vernon sat on horseback in the yard.

"What are you doing here?" Christine demanded without even an attempt at civility.

Vernon grinned lazily as he urged his horse closer. I took a deep breath, and felt the world settle into stillness around me.

This man knew what had happened to Griffin. Possibly was even responsible for it.

The wind rose, stirring up a dust devil in the yard. The horse balked at the sudden swirl of dust, but its rider didn't share the horse's protective instincts.

"Looking at you, I figure them doctors must be right," Vernon said, eyeing me in a most insolent fashion. "A man must have some kind of sickness of the brain, wanting to fuck something like you."

The water in the nearby trough began to churn, and the scars on my arm ached. "Where is Griffin?" I asked, and the words fell from my lips like frost.

"And Kander," Christine added. I could feel the tension radiating from her, her rage like a heat against my side.

"Your Arab fellow should've stayed in Egypt. As for Flaherty, he's exactly where he belongs." Vernon's grin sharpened. "At the poor farm, in the jail with the other lunatics."

My heart pumped liquid fear through my veins in place of blood. A glance at Christine's face showed her skin gone utterly white, her dark eyes like holes.

They were at the poor farm. Where Creigh would surely corrupt them both.

Thanks to the actions of this small-minded fool.

My vision tightened into a tunnel, with Vernon at the end of it. "You will give them back," I said, "or I will destroy you and everything you have ever loved."

Vernon's horse whinnied and tried to prance away. He reined it in sharply. "Don't think so." he sneered down at us. "In fact, that's the fate we have in mind for—"

A reddish ball of fury exploded from around the side of the barn. Vernon's horse, already spooked, reared in terror. Squawking at the top of his lungs, Diablo attacked.

The horse bolted, Vernon clinging to its back, half-unseated. Diablo flapped after them down the lane, until the horse finally outpaced him. Satisfied with his victory, the rooster strutted back to us, then stood and looked up with a beady eye.

The commotion brought Mr. Reynolds around the side of the barn at full speed. "What's going on? Was that Vernon Harper?"

"Indeed. I must say, your rooster has for once chosen a worthy target." I took the bread from my pocket and tossed the crumbs to Diablo. "Good creature of the fiery pit."

Reynolds frowned. "What did Vernon want?"

"Griffin and Iskander are in trouble," I replied, somewhat evasively, but it was easier than trying to explain the situation.

"Oh no." Reynolds paled beneath his tan. "What can I do to help?"

I hesitated, tempted by his offer. But he had a wife and three children.

And hadn't I ruined enough lives already? No sense in adding another good man to my account. "Look after your family." I nodded to the house. "After sunset, don't unlock the doors for anyone."

"But the community dance is tonight," he protested. "I was just getting ready to go wash up so we could leave."

"To the devil with the dance!" Christine exclaimed. Reynolds winced at her language.

Probably the Reynolds would be safe from attack. Unless Creigh believed we'd told them about her secrets.

Blast.

"Christine is right," I said. "It's not safe to travel after dark tonight."

Reynolds gave me a thoughtful look. "Does this have to do with the case Griffin is working on?"

I seized on the explanation. "Yes. I wish I could say more, but it isn't my place."

"Annie and the boys will be powerful disappointed to stay home tonight," he said unhappily. "But there will be other dances, and I ain't going to risk them if you say it ain't safe." He wavered, then added, "Annie's pretty good with the gun. If Griffin and Iskander are in trouble, I don't want to just sit by if I can help. She can look after the boys while I come with you."

I'd dragged enough innocents into horror and death. "That's very good of you," I said. "But no."

Christine nodded. "Thank you, though. You're a good man."

He looked to the house and sighed. "Guess I'd best break the news to Annie and the boys. Shout if you need anything."

"We will," I assured him.

Christine waited until the door shut behind him. "It's a trap, of course," she said. "With Griffin and Iskander as the bait."

"Obviously." I twisted my wedding ring on my finger, but it gave me no comfort. "But we can't simply leave them in Creigh's hands."

"No." Her mouth pressed into a taut line. "If she's hurt them…"

"Yes," I agreed. I turned and looked to the setting sun. "We'll sneak back under cover of darkness, as we did last night. And this time, we won't leave until the Fideles have been stopped. One way or another."

CHAPTER 23

Griffin

I SAT ON the hard concrete floor of the poor farm's jail, my body aching and my heart thumping against my ribs. All the corrupted who had been imprisoned here last night were gone, and I was alone. My hands were tied behind my back, although I had no means of picking the lock on the cell door even if I'd been free. The small, barred window, set high above my head, was too tiny to crawl through.

Every inch of me ached from the beating I'd received. Each movement I made found some new pain, from the deep bruises in my back to the sharp sting as hair matted into blood pulled against the wound in my scalp. Even so, nothing seemed to be broken, and I still had all of my teeth. Doubtless I had Iskander's intervention to thank for escaping as lightly as I had.

Iskander. A part of me wished he'd run and left me to my fate. They'd dragged him away when we arrived at the poor farm, taking him in the direction of the main house. What they'd done with him there, I didn't know and feared to find out. Equally, I feared to discover what they had planned for me. No one had tried to feed me any of the corrupted food, but surely it was only a matter of time. And when they did…then what? Would Creigh send me back to the Reynolds farm? Turn me into a weapon against my Ival?

I couldn't allow it. But how could I prevent it? Would the corruption let me warn him, or would Creigh compel me to silence? To wait until we were alone, until he was vulnerable, and then strike?

Ma had tried to prevent Vernon from bringing me here. I clung to that fact as tightly as I could.

Vernon. He'd told me I'd pay for what I'd done, in the same words the corrupted had used. There had to be a connection.

Ma thought God had inspired him to drill for water in the fallow place. Thanks to Delancey's letter and photos, I already knew the Fideles were behind it, but I'd assumed Vernon ignorant of their true nature. But what if he wasn't? What if he knew everything?

It would explain why none of the corrupted corn from the field had found its way onto their table. Why he'd made sure to keep the house garden on the old well only.

But Marian was corrupted. Had there been some kind of mistake? Did he even know?

Or perhaps I was wrong. I didn't want to believe it of him. Didn't want to think the little boy who had hidden beneath a table with me, or played at soldiers in his yard, would willingly do such a thing.

There came the rattle of a key in the door. I stilled, waiting, and a moment later Mrs. Creigh stepped in.

Sorcery left a mark on those who practiced it. There was a light burning in her eyes—a mere flicker compared to Whyborne's incandescence, but enough for my shadowsight to perceive. She had touched the arcane, had bent the world to her will.

"Let us go," I said, before she could speak. "If you know what happened in Widdershins last July, then you know Whyborne isn't an enemy you want to make. Neither is Christine, for that matter."

Creigh tilted her head to one side. "Mr. Delancey believed the Fideles made a mistake. That we should have followed the Cabal's lead and recruited Dr. Whyborne instead of his brother."

Could I possibly get some useful information from her? It seemed worth a try. "Whyborne wasn't recruited by the Cabal," I said. "They were in touch with him through one of their members, nothing more."

"I'm quite aware of the situation, Mr. Flaherty. Many of the sorcerers in the Cabal also belong to the Fideles." She arched a brow at my surprise. "Really, where do you think most sorcerers get their power and knowledge from?"

"The Man in the Woods," I said numbly. God. I should have thought of it before. "Reverend Scarrow was killed by one of the Cabal, wasn't he? Someone he trusted?"

"Probably." She shrugged. "His death unsettled Mr. Delancey— who was himself both a member of the Cabal and the Fideles. I should have recognized it as a sign of weakness and had him dealt with before his case of cold feet became terminal. At first I cursed Odell for not dealing with him quickly enough, for giving us away." Her mouth twitched into a smile that sent a wash of cold down my back. "Now I realize it was an opportunity."

"You mean to corrupt Whyborne," I said, ashes in my mouth. "You gave Miss Norton the pumpkin, didn't you? And now you mean to use me as bait."

"Yes, yes." She waved a dismissive hand. "But I'm not here because of Dr. Whyborne. I'm far more interested in you." She cocked her head. "Why is it that Mrs. Harper is so *very* insistent we not infect you?"

No. She couldn't be saying what I thought. "Marian?"

But Marian was corrupted. Marian was a victim of what the Fideles had wrought.

Wasn't she?

"I could insist, of course," Creigh went on, ignoring my shock. "But why bother? Dear Marian has been…temperamental…as of late. I could simply enforce my will on her, but I find it's much easier to make suggestions to a partner than compel a slave. If letting her devise some worse fate for you settles her down, then I'm happy to go along with her little plan. You'll serve as bait for Dr. Whyborne just as effectively either way."

"You're lying," I said, because it didn't make any sense. What did Creigh mean by suggestions to a partner? She was a powerful sorceress, and Marian the simple wife of a farmer.

Or perhaps I'd underestimated Marian from the start.

"Why would I lie?" Creigh asked. She fingered the jewel at her throat absently. "What I want to know is this. You know the truth about this world. So why do you oppose us?"

I sat back, and winced at the pain shooting through my back. "Because I have some allegiance to humanity?" I suggested.

"Allegiance to humanity?" She let out a hiss of impatience. "You idiot. Why do you think I'm doing any of this to begin with? The masters are going to return whether I wish them to or not. When last they left, humanity was no threat to them. We were beneath their notice, save as raw materials. What do you think their response will be when they return to discover our cities? Our great ships plying the oceans? To find we've covered almost every corner of the globe?"

"Which is why we must fight them!"

Creigh let out an unladylike snort. "Fight them? How? The masters *created* the maelstrom beneath Widdershins. They twisted the very arcane lines of the earth to make a vortex of immense power, dwarfing all others. Do you imagine, even for an instant, that you can foil the will of creatures capable of such a feat?"

My mouth felt dry, but I kept my gaze defiant. "The umbrae rebelled."

"And were sealed in their cities."

"The ketoi rebelled as well."

"And they will surely be punished for their defiance." Creigh folded her arms across her chest. "Humanity cannot win a war against the masters. The best we can hope for is to prove our usefulness, so they don't wipe our entire species from the face of the earth."

I didn't bother to hide my contempt. "And the fact you're enslaving the men and women of the poor farm, infecting them to accumulate your own power? Don't pretend you act out of charity."

"The rust is but one tool of the masters, abandoned when they left." Creigh smiled. "There are others. Don't imagine the Fideles are not busy elsewhere as well. The Restoration *will* take place. You cannot win." She tilted her head. "Perhaps it's just as well you won't live to see it."

She left in a swirl of skirts. As the door locked behind her, I slumped forward in my bonds and prayed.

CHAPTER 24

Whyborne

CHRISTINE AND I went on foot to the poor farm.

We'd considered taking the wagon—Lawrence would have gladly lent it—but I didn't want to deprive the family of what might be their only chance for escape, should they need it. Instead, we armed ourselves as best we could and set out with the lowering of the sun.

Christine had brought her rifle and all the ammunition she could carry. In the dark, we might find a place where she could lay low and pick off the corrupted from a distance. And if not, or if Creigh threatened her with the fire spell, she'd brought an old scythe as a weapon. Though no longer used in modern farming, Lawrence had kept it as something of a memento in the barn. Now its edge gleamed from recent sharpening, and from the intent look on her face, I knew Christine wouldn't hesitate to use it against anyone who dared get between her and Iskander.

I carried a lantern, extra kerosene, and Griffin's lock picking tools. It seemed likely he and Iskander would be held in the jail, and though I might be able to remove the outer door by force, opening the cells without injuring the captives would require more finesse.

And if I stepped inside and found them already transforming into the cinereous form of the corrupted, as the previous captives had...

I'd burn it all down, and wipe the whole accursed town from the map.

We didn't speak, merely strode down the empty road side-by-side. In the distance, the light of lanterns bathed a large barn. No doubt that was where the community dance was even now underway.

Creigh wouldn't be there, but Vernon likely would. Smiling and strutting, while Creigh did God knew what to Griffin and Iskander...

There came a rustling from a low hedge not far before us. Christine and I both froze, and I lifted the lantern warily. Was it animal or ambush?

A human figure emerged, and for a moment I thought Creigh had sent the corrupted to lay in wait for us. Christine hefted the scythe, and the frost spell hovered on my tongue.

"Christine!" Iskander cried. "Hold up—it's me!"

He looked the worse for wear: his suit torn and one eye blackening. Christine let out a glad cry, dropped the scythe, and ran to him. He caught her up in his arms, and they clung to one another.

No one else emerged from the hedge. Griffin wasn't with him.

"Where is Griffin?" I asked urgently.

Iskander and Christine stepped apart, though she kept a hand on his arm. "Still captive, I'm afraid." Iskander shook his head angrily. "It was Vernon—he captured us at the Kerr farm and took us to Creigh. We were separated once there. I don't know where they took Griffin— the jail, I assume. I was locked in one of the bedrooms on the upper floor of the big house."

Christine frowned. "Why separate the two of you?"

"Sod if I know." He glanced from her to me. "Whatever they had planned for me, I wasn't about to wait around for it. I stripped the beds, tied the sheets into a rope, and lowered myself from the window. As soon as my feet touched the ground, I ran." He winced. "I'm terribly sorry, Whyborne. I feel a coward for abandoning Griffin as I did, but I was at a loss as to see how I might free him by myself, without getting recaptured. And I had to let you know of the trap."

"Of course," Christine said staunchly. "There was nothing else you could have done, Kander."

An unjust part of me wanted to insist otherwise. Say that Iskander shouldn't have deserted Griffin, left him alone to be corrupted. But the reaction was irrational. "Christine is right. How would you even have gotten into the jail, with the door locked? You would only have been caught."

He nodded. "Thank you, old chap. And, as I said, I needed to warn you."

Christine let go of him and retrieved her scythe. "Really, Kander, how stupid do you think we are? Of *course* it's a trap. But we can't just leave Griffin in Creigh's hands."

"That's what I mean. Griffin isn't at the poor farm anymore."

I frowned. "What are you talking about?"

Iskander ran his hand back through his thick hair. He looked tired, and dust clung to suit and skin. "I overheard Creigh and Mr. Tate speaking in the house. They must have been just below me; if I pressed my ear against a knothole in the floor, I could make out what they were saying. Creigh and her army of corrupted are waiting for you at the poor farm. But Tate is conducting some sort of-of fiendish ritual at the fallow place."

Alarm leached the warmth from my extremities. "Ritual?"

"I don't know what. It has something to do with the rust—that's what they call the corruption." Iskander's dark eyes looked black in the dim light of the lantern. "Something to make it spread, perhaps? I couldn't make that part out. But it involves blood, Whyborne."

"Oh God," I said numbly. "They mean to sacrifice Griffin."

CHAPTER 25

Griffin

I STUMBLED OVER the sheared corn stalks toward the fallow place, with only the grip of the corrupted on either arm to keep me from falling.

The sun had slipped below the horizon in a glorious blaze of red, gold, and darkest blue. The dust kicked up by the last of the harvesters filled my nose, along with the scent of corn sap. At any other time, I would have called it a beautiful evening; the perfect time to sit out on the porch with a cigar and a whiskey, and watch the stars come out.

Instead, I feared the evening would end with my death.

What had become of Iskander, I didn't know. I asked Creigh when she returned shortly before sundown to open my cell, but of course she'd given me no answer. Her corrupted took hold of me and dragged me out of the jail and away from the cluster of buildings without explanation.

But why? She'd meant me to serve as bait in a trap for Whyborne. Wasn't it enough that he thought me in the jail?

The windmill at the new well turned lazily in the breeze, metal blades squeaking with every revolution. No doubt the Fideles meant to use the water to infect later harvests as well. The winter wheat, the spring wheat, next year's crop of corn, all poison to be shipped east, first to Widdershins, then elsewhere. Philadelphia, Washington, New York…there was no end to the havoc they might cause, the powerful men they might put under their control.

An old scarecrow stood near the windmill's base, hauled from wherever it had originally stood and planted here. The corrupted dragged me to it. I tried to struggle, but there were too many of them. Shortly thereafter I found myself tied to the scarecrow, my arms outspread. I yanked against my bindings, but they didn't give.

Shapes emerged from the darkness. The cinereous, their bodies devoured by the rust from the inside out, their wet skin swollen from the corruption within. The only figure free of its touch was a man I assumed must be Mr. Tate. A bit to my surprise, he wasn't marked by either sorcery or corruption. Indeed, he looked pale and dazed, almost as though he wasn't quite certain how he'd come to be here.

And after him came Vernon and Marian.

"At last," Marian said. She pulled her bonnet off, letting it fall to the ground.

The sight thus revealed turned my blood to ice. Two small nubs, like the first growth of antlers on a deer, jutted from her forehead. The tips glowed with magic, even in the glare of the great arcane line.

Was this yet a third form of the corruption?

She stared at me almost gleefully, her eyes burning bright with hatred. "You're going to suffer, Griffin Flaherty," she said. "After all these years, you'll finally pay for what you did."

Oh God. Those words hadn't belonged to the Fideles, hadn't been uttered at Creigh's command. They'd come from Marian.

Vernon put a hand to her waist. "Yes he will, my dear."

The cinereous came to a halt just within the circle of light. My mouth had gone dry with fear, but I forced my voice to remain calm. "Marian, I don't know what you think I've done, but it isn't worth this."

"I'll be the judge of that." Marian tilted her head back slightly to look up at me. "You destroyed Benjamin, Griffin. You took him away from me." She grinned, but there was no humor in it. "And now you get to watch while I take your lover from you."

Oh God. Whatever Vernon's motives, Marian had entered into

some unholy bargain with Creigh looking for revenge. "We never meant to hurt you—" I started.

"Shut up!" She took a step toward me, her hands curling into fists. "You knew we were engaged, but you couldn't keep your hands to yourself. It's thanks to *you* this filthy town discovered his secret." She held up her hand as I tried to protest. "But we managed to get past that. I loved him. And he loved me."

"I'm sure he did," I said. And I even meant it. Benjamin and I had been young and stupid, but he'd cared about Marian even then. There was no reason their relationship couldn't have bloomed into love.

"We put it behind us," she said. "Benjamin promised to be faithful to me, and he was. But the rest of the community wouldn't let it go. The anonymous letters, the barely veiled references in the papers, the sneering sermons by that damned parson, hounded him to his death!"

"No!" cried a voice from the darkness.

To my utter horror, Ma stepped into the light. She clutched an old shotgun in her shaking hands, and her eyes were wide. She looked terrified, and my heart clenched. No doubt she'd seen the lights, the movement, in the field and come to investigate. To drive away the prowlers she and everyone else believed stalked the town after dark.

"Aunt Nella, go back to the house," Vernon ordered. He took hold of the gun, and she let him pull it away without resistance.

"I don't know what's going on here," she said, her voice trembling as badly as her hands. Her eyes darted wildly to the cinereous, and she swallowed convulsively. "But let Griffin go. If you've got to be mad at someone, Marian, be mad at me."

"And why should I do that?" Marian asked.

Ma closed her eyes. "Because it was my fault, what happened to your first husband. I'm the one who wrote the letters."

CHAPTER 26

Whyborne

ISKANDER HAD BEEN right. We'd extinguished our lantern well back, and crept slowly through the shorn corn fields, careful to avoid the irrigation ditches. Fallen leaves and husks, dried by the sun, crunched under our feet, but I could only hope it wouldn't be enough to give us away. At least out in the open, we could be certain there were no corrupted lying in ambush amidst the rows.

We'd seen the light at the base of the windmill from some distance. But now, we were just near enough to make out a few dark figures moving about.

"Here," Iskander whispered hoarsely. We crouched by him at the edge of one of the irrigation ditches, careful not to touch the water. "Look—what are they doing?"

I leaned forward, straining my eyes. Christine did the same. "Good gad," she gasped, "is that Griffin? Tied to a scarecrow?"

Horror stabbed through me. This must be part of whatever foul ritual Tate had planned. They'd sacrifice Griffin to the hellish thing infesting the water, use his blood to do…what?

"We have to get down there," I said urgently. "Before they harm him further."

"Agreed," Christine said. "Can you use your magic on the water in the well? Cause it to flood out and knock them over?"

I didn't like the idea of scattering the tainted water near Griffin, assuming he hadn't been corrupted already. Still, it would certainly be safer than setting fire to the field. "All right," I said. "Christine, you stay back and get ready to shoot. Iskander, take the scythe."

Something hard and cold pressed against the back of my neck. Christine let out a startled gasp.

"That's quite all right," Iskander said. "I'm already armed."

~ * ~

I turned my head as far as I dared, and saw all the blood drain from Christine's face. Iskander pressed the bore of a pistol to the base of her skull with one hand; the other hand held a second pistol against my neck.

"Don't move," he advised us.

"Kander, no," Christine said, her voice barely above a whisper. "Oh God, no."

He'd been corrupted the whole evening. There had been a trap, all right, and we'd followed him right into its jaws. Was there even a ritual planned, or was it all just set dressing to trick us into letting down our guard?

My mind raced. Fire was out—exploding either gun would likely kill all three of us, even if harming Iskander hadn't been out of the question. Frost? I could only concentrate on one gun at a time. If he dropped one, he might pull the other trigger before I could cast the spell a second time. What orders had Creigh given him, exactly? Were both of us to be captured, or was Christine expendable?

"Fight it, Kander," Christine urged. "This isn't you! Creigh is controlling your mind, but I know you. You can fight it off. You can come back to me."

The guns didn't waver. There came a sloshing sound, and a moment later, four of the cinereous rose from the irrigation ditch, where they'd lain hidden beneath the water.

Within moments, they'd seized us and hauled us upright. Iskander unshuttered the lantern, keeping one pistol trained on us at all times. His eyes looked flat and black in the light, all trace of his usual liveliness gone.

"Kander," Christine tried again.

He ignored her plea while he disarmed us both. Then he led the way toward the windmill, while the cinereous dragged us helplessly behind.

CHAPTER 27

Griffin

"MA?" I WHISPERED.

The world seemed to have stilled to a point. What Ma had just said was impossible. She might not have approved of me, and certainly not of Whyborne, but she wasn't cruel. She'd never do such an abominable thing.

Marian's eyes widened, and she sagged against Vernon. "N-Nella?"

Ma wrung her hands together, her own gaze downcast. "I'm sorry! I'm so sorry. But don't you see? Benjamin took away my boy, my only son." She swallowed convulsively. "I'd raised Griffin right; I knew I had, because he always *did* right. Never did anything to make me ashamed, not once. So what happened—it had to be Benjamin's fault."

I hadn't imagined my spirits could sink any lower. What a fool I'd been.

"I was so angry at him," Ma went on. "It wasn't fair! Why did he get to stay here in Fallow, when my boy was exiled? Why did he get to carry on with his life, while Griffin had to leave, to go to the city where he didn't know a soul in the world? Why did Benjamin's ma get to see her son whenever she wanted, and I had to be content with letters and postcards?"

Marian straightened slowly. "No."

I heard the edge of warning in her voice, but Ma continued on. "He couldn't just get away with it. So I started sending him letters. One every month, just to remind him that someone knew he'd escaped just punishment. And I sent them to the papers too, every year or so, to make sure no one else forgot it, either."

"No," I whispered, denying it.

"No," Marian growled, fury flashing in her eyes.

"I never thought it would hurt him!" Ma cried, raising her gaze at last. Tears streamed down her face. "I thought he was—was laughing because he got away with it. That he didn't care what had happened to Griffin. I thought he didn't care about anything, that he was just the worst kind of sinner, without remorse. And then...and then..."

Then Benjamin killed himself.

"You were kind to me," Marian said, and if she'd been a sorceress, the very air would have frozen around us. "After Benjamin died, you were the only soul in this damned town that cared. And you were the one who killed him!"

"I didn't mean to!" Ma put her hands over her eyes. "When I realized what I'd done, I would've given anything to take it back. The least I could do was look out for you. And when Vernon came, and you two got married, I was so happy. I thought maybe I'd made up for it by giving you a new husband to replace the old one. Maybe God could forgive me."

"God doesn't forgive, you bitch," Marian snarled. "And neither do I!"

"Stop!" I shouted as she lunged at Ma.

"Enough!" Creigh rested one hand on the jewel at her throat. It flashed in my shadowsight—and so did the antler-like stubs on Marian's forehead.

Marian stumbled to a halt, her fingers hooked into claws. A look of utter frenzy crossed her face, but she seemed powerless to disobey.

"I tire of this pointless family drama," Creigh went on. "I've indulged you so far because of your assistance, but don't forget who is truly in control. You might be the avatar, but I am the master." She smiled faintly. "So to speak."

"This isn't...I agreed to all this to save the town," Tate said, looking troubled.

"And that is exactly what we will do, Mr. Tate," Creigh said. "I'm sure you agree we have more important things to deal with than petty squabbles." She gestured, and I saw the light of a lantern making its way toward us.

Iskander held it, and I bit back a cry of horror at the sight of gray corruption blighting his bronze skin. And behind him, in the grip of two cinereous, were Whyborne and Christine.

CHAPTER 28

Whyborne

MY HEART POUNDED madly as the cinereous dragged us into the torch-lit circle. The windmill loomed overhead, some bearing within squeaking with every revolution of the blades. Creigh stood smirking in triumph, an uncertain looking Tate beside her. Vernon was there, the bastard, as was Marian, her expression one of murderous fury. And what the devil was sprouting from her head? It almost looked like the beginnings of horns, or antlers, furred with black mold rather than velvet.

Nella cringed next to Griffin, her eyes wide with terror and her face streaked with tears.

My gaze met Griffin's, read the fear in his emerald eyes. They'd bound him to a scarecrow, either because it was convenient, or because it had been a bit of set dressing for the lie about the sacrifice.

The lie Iskander had told. I didn't dare look in Christine's direction.

If Griffin was bound, did that mean he wasn't corrupted? Certainly he appeared terrified, and there seemed no reason for such a charade now. God, if only I had his shadowsight. I would have seen Iskander's corruption and kept us out of this trap. Perhaps even turned the tables on Creigh.

Creigh touched the stone at her throat. "Bring Dr. Whyborne to me," she ordered.

The cinereous dragged me to her—then shoved me roughly to my knees.

"Stop!" Griffin shouted, and the fear in his voice tore at my heart. "Let him go!"

"You're going to be sorry!" Christine bellowed.

"I think not." Creigh's eyes gleamed as she looked down at me. "Quite the opposite, actually. Widdershins is too critical to leave in the hands of a rogue sorcerer with no allegiance to anyone save himself. You might have bowed to the masters willingly, hybrid. Now, you will bow whether you wish to or not."

No. I had to do something—anything.

I reached for the water in the well, the plan Christine and I had made now a matter of desperation. I felt the water begin to surge, the world respond—

Then Marian lifted a languid hand.

The spell drained away from my grasp—not unraveled like on the edge of a witch hunter's blade, but just…gone.

Griffin gasped in shock—no doubt his shadowsight revealed whatever had happened.

I tried again, putting more power into it. But again, the spell drained away, like water through my fingers.

"Keep at it," Marian said with a grin. "I'm hungry."

Hungry? Was she absorbing the spells somehow? The corruption in her feeding on their energy? None of the other corrupted had shown any ability to do anything like that.

Something was clearly different about Marian. But what? And why?

There was no time to figure it out. Tate had gone to the well pump while Marian toyed with me. Now he returned, carrying a cup of water.

No.

"No!" Griffin cried. "Don't! *Ival!*"

I fixed a glare on Creigh, determined to give nothing away. "This will do you no good," I told her. "You won't be able to fool my friends and family back in Widdershins. They'll realize something is wrong."

"Just as you noticed something wrong with your friend?" Creigh asked with a smirk.

"I'm sorry, Dr. Whyborne," Tate said. "Fallow is dying—will die if we can't ship the corn east. This is the only way to save the town."

The cinereous seized my head as Tate approached with the infected water. I struggled against their grip, but they were too many, too strong.

"Ival!" Griffin called from somewhere behind me, and oh God I wished I could see him one last time, while my mind was still my own. "I love you!"

Then they forced my mouth open, and Tate poured the water down my throat.

CHAPTER 29

Griffin

IVAL'S STRUGGLES CEASED. He hung in the grip of the cinereous, while the rust worked its horror on him. I longed to close my eyes, to look away, not watch this happen to my love. But it would feel like an abandonment if I did.

My shadowsight revealed the grayish black lines spreading over his skin. The scars on his arm seemed to attract the corruption; they flushed dark, all the way to the very tips of his fingers.

"No," I whispered helplessly. Tears slicked my cheeks, but I was bound tight, and I couldn't even wipe them away.

"I'm going to kill every last one of you," Christine said, her voice shaking with a mixture of rage and grief.

Creigh and Tate ignored her. "Let him go," Creigh ordered.

The cinereous released their hold on him. Ival fell to his hands and knees, head bowed. I couldn't see his face anymore, couldn't see the black tendrils creeping across his beloved features.

Marian let out a low, ugly laugh. "How does it feel, Griffin?" she taunted. "What should I have him do first? Kill your friend? Or no."

Her gaze fixed on Ma, who shrank against me. "Your mother deserves to die."

"Silence," Creigh snapped. "You forget who is in command here. *I* shall decide what use to make of Dr. Whyborne."

Ival laughed.

It was a strange sound, nothing like his usual reserved chuckle. His whole body jerked, and then…

And then he *burned.*

It was nothing anyone else could see, but my shadowsight revealed the rush of magical fire. It started in his fingertips, touching the earth beneath which ran the arcane line. The black-clotted scars were stark against his skin…

And then the black began to crumble, to flake away, replaced by blue fire.

Marian let out a cry, almost of pain.

Creigh frowned, not yet alarmed. "What is he doing?" She glanced back at Marian—then seemed to realize something was truly wrong. "Stop him this instant!"

"Stop me?" Ival asked in a voice like something ancient, something that lay within the earth and the sea. His body convulsed, and he coughed, expelling a cloud of black dust.

The rust, burned to ash.

"Stop *me?*" he repeated, louder this time. "Do. You. Know. What. I. Am?"

He surged to his feet, his movements slightly jerky, as if he didn't quite fit his own body anymore. When he turned on us, his eyes blazed with blue fire even in my ordinary sight. Creigh let out a gasp of shock. "Seize him!"

"Do you know what I am?" he howled in that ancient voice. The cloth above his scars began to char into ashes. "I am the fire that burns in the veins of the world! I am the maelstrom made flesh!" He dropped into a crouch, slamming his palm against the barren earth. "How *dare* you touch me, filthy parasite?"

The arcane line exploded in my vision, forcing me to look away. Power howled through the field, and I could feel it against my skin like a blast of hot wind. Something roared beneath the ground, answered by a scream of agony from Marian. Both were nearly drowned out by the warning shriek of overstressed metal. The windmill swayed madly —then water surged from the well, smashing wood and steel to flinders.

"Look out!" shouted Tate.

The windmill struck the ground in a twisted heap. Water pooled around it—but no trace remained of the spores. The arcane fire had burned away the rust beneath the ground.

I felt hands plucking against my bindings. Startled, I looked down, and found Ma working at the ropes with shaking fingers.

Vernon held Marian, who looked dazed. Creigh and Tate were distracted, but they wouldn't remain so for long. They'd realize they could still use us as hostages against Ival, and Ma couldn't free me fast enough to prevent it.

And I wasn't going to let them turn me into a weapon against him a second time.

"Ival!" I yelled. "The stone! Use the curse breaking spell on it, now!"

He staggered a bit as he rose, but kept his feet. Creigh grabbed the stone and it pulsed. The protrusions on Marian's forehead pulsed in answer.

The cinereous released Christine, rushing toward Whyborne. Without hesitation, Christine seized a steel rod from the fallen windmill and attacked the cinereous from behind. The rod sank deep into their soft flesh with every blow, leaving behind dents as she wrested it free. It didn't stop them, but it slowed them just long enough for Whyborne to reach Creigh.

Creigh stumbled away, but Whyborne was faster and seized her wrist. Before she could fight back with some magic, the arcane energy flared once again.

There was no finesse to what he did, not this time. He grasped the jewel in his hand and simply tore the spell into shreds.

The cinereous making for Whyborne stopped in their tracks. Perhaps encouraged by their stillness, Christine began to beat them with even more force.

The bindings around one of my wrists came undone. I began to frantically untie the knot around my other wrist, as Ma attacked the rope securing my legs to the scarecrow's pole. I held my breath, expecting Iskander or the cinereous to attack us at any moment.

But they didn't. None of them moved, or showed the slightest interest in anything happening in front of them.

Creigh raked her nails across Whyborne's face. He released her, and she staggered back. "This means nothing," she snarled. "Marian —stop him!"

Marian laughed softly, and the sound turned my blood cold.

"You think to order me?" she said, a triumphant grin twisting her features. Was it my imagination, or were the antler-like growths on her forehead getting longer? "Now that the spell of control is destroyed, why should I listen?"

"You treacherous bitch!" Creigh shouted. "You're nothing but a tool! Without me to guide you—"

Vernon laughed. "Oh, I think my Marian can guide herself," he said, putting a hand to her waist. "Especially since she had the brilliant idea of providing several of the dishes for the community dance, even though we couldn't go ourselves."

Horror closed my throat. The dance. Everyone in Fallow would be there, from editor Carson to Lawrence and Annie, from the oldest man to the youngest child.

"I've felt them come into my control all evening," Marian said. "They're mine now, to do whatever I want with. Revenge at last, and I have you to thank for it."

"No!" shouted Tate. "My wife, my daughter were there! You have to let them go. You can't do this!"

The last of my bindings gave way. I fell to the ground. If we could just get away while they were distracted, perhaps—

"Parasite," Whyborne snarled. He paced toward Marian, a blaze of light in my vision.

Marian turned to him, and an odd look of glee crossed her face. "*You.* I didn't see you, hiding in that pathetic skin. What *are* you?" She licked her lips, and the corruption unfurled around her like wings. "You'll make the perfect celebratory dinner."

Then she struck.

Whyborne tried to pull on the magic of the arcane line, but he was spent. In a moment, she was on him. The dark arms of the corruption snatched his spells from the air—and then speared directly into him.

His mouth stretched open in a soundless cry, and his back arched. Dear God, what was she *doing* to him?

"Yes," she groaned. "I never realized. They've kept me in famine, when I could have had a feast!" Her eyes widened with revelation. "But this is nothing compared to the vortex they spoke of. The one in Widdershins. If I could feed on it, I would be unstoppable."

Tate pulled a revolver from his pocket and leveled it at Marian.

There came the roar of a gun. Tate jerked back, blood coating his vest. Iskander lowered the pistol he'd used to shoot Tate, looking utterly unconcerned by his own actions.

Vernon laughed. "I guess you shouldn't have underestimated us after all," he said.

Then he staggered forward. Creigh stood behind his fallen body, her expression wild and desperate. In her hands, she clutched a length of wood from the windmill, which she'd used to strike him.

Marian jerked, her attention distracted from Whyborne. "Vernon!"

I couldn't hesitate, couldn't think. Whyborne lay motionless on the ground, and I ran to him. "Christine! Leave off and help me!"

"Kander!" She dropped the metal rod and grabbed her husband.

And he grabbed her in return, his hand closing mercilessly over her wrist.

Then he staggered as Creigh struck him as well. "Come on!" she gasped. "Tate's wagon is this way!"

Christine hesitated, visibly torn. "You can't help him if you're corrupted too," Creigh snapped. "And if we try to take him with us, Marian will know where we are instantly. Either come on, or stay here and join him!"

The cinereous began to shamble toward us.

Christine swore, scooped up one of Iskander's dropped pistols, and ran to me. Between us, we hefted Whyborne's weight on our shoulders. Spasms wracked his body, nearly tearing him from our grasp.

"Come on, Ma!" I shouted.

She came, and Creigh, the four of us stumbling along, dragging Whyborne with us. Christine twisted around and fired, picking off the nearest of the cinereous.

Somehow, we reached the road just ahead of our pursuers. Creigh led the way to a horse-drawn wagon. "Hurry!" she shouted. Christine swung up beside her, and pressed the pistol into Creigh's side.

"So much as look like you might betray us, and I'll blow you straight to hell," Christine warned.

I heaved Whyborne into the bed of the wagon, helped Ma up, then leapt in after them. Even as the cinereous reached the road, Creigh snapped the reins. "Hee-yah!"

The horses sprang into motion. Then we were gaining speed, the cart careening madly along the road. I shifted Ival's head into my lap and clung to the side of the wagon as we left the fields behind.

CHAPTER 30

Griffin

WHYBORNE'S BODY ARCHED, his heels drumming against the wagon bed. "He's having a seizure!" I cried, and grabbed him by the shoulders. "Ma, hold his legs!"

To my relief, she did as asked without question. Whyborne thrashed in our grip, spine bending and eyes rolling.

"What the devil did Marian do to him?" Christine shouted. I glanced up to see her dig the barrel of the gun into Creigh's side. "Tell us!"

"I don't know!" Creigh exclaimed. Her pale face was drawn, but her eyes remained fixed on the road ahead. "What *is* he?"

"*I am the fire that burns in the veins of the world!*" he'd shouted. "*I am the maelstrom made flesh!*"

"He's our friend," Christine growled. "And it's thanks to you Kander is corrupted and Whyborne injured! Give me one good reason I shouldn't shoot you and dump your body in the road for the vultures to find?"

"Because Marian is out of control and wants to kill us all now,"

Creigh said with remarkable composure. "Keep her from murdering me, and I'll tell you anything you wish to know."

Whyborne's body heaved against my grip—and his eyes flew open. "Griffin," he said between gritted teeth.

"Yes," I said. God, what was happening to him? "Come back to me, Ival, please."

He blinked rapidly—then suddenly his eyes burned with arcane fire, and I nearly jerked back from the shock of it.

"Can you see me, Griffin?" he demanded in the voice of something ancient.

I tightened my grip on him. "Yes, I see you, Ival," I assured him. "I'm here."

"I found you." His fingers scrabbled at my wrists. "I saw you. Broken, perfect, beautiful, fractured, Griffin, do you see me? Do you see me; *do you see me?*"

"Yes!" I dug my fingers into his shoulders, desperate that he hear me, that he understand. "I see you!"

"What's wrong with him?" Ma asked sounding frightened.

"Slap him a few times," Christine suggested.

I ignored them both and cupped Whyborne's face in my hands. "I see you," I repeated, since he seemed fixated on the idea. "I see you, my dear."

"Yes." His eyes drifted shut. "You've always seen me. That's why I brought you home."

The tension left his shoulders. I shook him slightly, but received no response. "He's lost consciousness." I looked up at Creigh. "What did Marian do to him?"

"I already told you, I don't know." She let the horses slow and glanced back at us. "The rust feeds on arcane power. That's how it survived the millennia—it latched onto the arcane line and fed enough to keep itself alive. It's how Marian can devour spells. But she was feeding directly on him, which shouldn't be possible, unless he's going about with arcane energy inside him."

I ran my fingers down the side of his face. "Fire in His Blood," I whispered. The name the ketoi gave to him.

The version of him I'd glimpsed in July, in those moments when he slipped free of mortal chains: burning in my sight the same way the maelstrom burned.

"I am the fire that burns in the veins of the world!"

"It doesn't matter now," Christine said. "Where are we going? And how are we to save Kander?"

"I don't yet know how to save him, but we will," I said. "We have to regroup first. Perhaps we could go to the Reynolds' farm. At least to get our things." I swallowed. "I suppose they're all corrupted now."

Christine shook her head. "Whyborne and I told them to stay home. They're safe."

Thank God. I closed my eyes and pressed my forehead to Whyborne's. Breathing his breath.

"And there's another thing you have to answer for," Christine said to Creigh. "Vernon's farm supplied the food to the community dance. Did you know about that?"

"What's going on?" Ma shouted abruptly. I looked up, and Christine fell silent. Even Creigh looked surprised.

"I'm sorry," she said, sitting back, "but I don't understand. All this seems like…like a terrible dream! I keep thinking I'll wake up."

I couldn't imagine how bizarre the evening must have seemed to her. "Magic is real, just as I tried to tell you earlier today. To summarize, Whyborne, Christine, Iskander and I are trying to keep the world from being plunged into darkness and humanity destroyed. Mrs. Creigh, Vernon, and Marian are on the other side."

"I already explained—oh never mind," Creigh snapped. "And I'd say it's clear Marian isn't on anyone's side but her own."

"She wanted revenge," I said. "For Benjamin's death." I looked at Ma, but she wouldn't meet my gaze.

"No man is worth that much effort," Creigh said with a sniff. "Power is far more reliable."

"Shut up," Christine said. "Griffin, I don't think we dare seek shelter with the Reynolds. I don't want to draw more trouble on them."

"Agreed." I tried to think. "We need somewhere relatively secure, where we can lie low and let Whyborne recover."

Ma cleared her throat. "The boarded up jewelry store?" she suggested tentatively. "They had all kinds of fancy alarms and locks when they were open for business. It ought to be secure."

"Brilliant, Ma," I said. "We'll have to take the wagon elsewhere and abandon it, so as not to draw attention. And the horses as well."

"Then what?" Creigh demanded. "That isn't much of a plan. We need to stop Marian! Didn't you hear her—she was talking about feeding on the vortex itself. If she reaches Widdershins, she'll spread the infection beyond the ability of anyone to control."

Whyborne's hair was soft beneath my fingers as I brushed the spiky locks back from his face. "If we're to stop her, we need Whyborne. Which means we have to wait for him to wake up," I said. And refused to give voice to the lingering fear that he might not wake up at all.

~ * ~

While Christine drove the horses and cart away, Creigh and I carried Whyborne upstairs to the small suite of rooms above the store. The previous owners had taken the more portable items with them when they left, but abandoned the larger pieces of furniture, including the bed. The fact that there weren't enough people left in Fallow to have stolen any of it drove home how close to the edge the town truly was. No wonder Tate had been desperate enough to become entangled with the Fideles.

Ma followed us upstairs and lingered, even when Creigh declared her intention to go down and wait for Christine's return. Although I knew I should keep an eye on Creigh's every movement, I couldn't bear to leave Ival's side. There were no sheets, so I stripped off my filthy coat and laid it over him.

He didn't move. Didn't blink. Didn't stir.

"Is he going to wake up?" Ma asked. She looked worn out from the last few hours, her gray hair come half out of its bun, her dress smudged and dirty.

"Yes." I stroked his cheek tenderly, not caring what she thought. Not caring about anything but him.

"How do you know?"

"Because the other option is unbearable." I sat back not knowing what, if anything, I owed her. Not after what she'd done. "You sent Benjamin the letters."

She dropped her eyes. "It was wrong of me."

It was more than wrong. It was monstrous.

She'd let her own pain blot out any possibility of his. Clung to her hurt to deny that he was capable of feeling anything.

What would the Mother of Shadows say, if I could speak to her now? She wouldn't agree with what Ma had done, that much I knew. The umbrae lacked the capacity for such cruelty.

"Why did you do it?" I asked. "Did you truly blame Benjamin for what we both did?"

Ma flinched. "I didn't see how you could...you were always my little boy. So sweet and loving, and never gave me a lick of trouble."

My lungs felt filled with glass, every breath sending slivers deeper. "And if I was able to desire men as well as women, then what? I couldn't be sweet or loving? Couldn't be a good person?"

"You heard the preacher the same as I did," she said raggedly. "The men of Sodom were wicked. Not like you at all. So I figured it must have been the Walter boy. He tempted you into something you'd never have done otherwise." Her breath caught, a quiet sob. "But then we came to Widdershins, and found out you were living with this one, and...and..."

And she could no longer imagine I had no desire for men. That Benjamin had somehow seduced me, convinced me to commit a sin I would never have considered on my own. "And you realized just how wrong you'd been?"

"No! I mean, I already knew. Back when Benjamin killed himself." She put her face in her hands. "But once I realized you were still...that you'd chosen..."

She'd felt even guiltier. "Men, Ma," I said tiredly. "I like men and women, both. I'm more inclined to men, but I won't pretend women leave me unmoved."

"Then why not marry?" she demanded, dropping her hands to stare pleadingly at me. "If not your cousin Ruth, then someone else? Why...this?"

She made it sound so easy. As if it wouldn't hurt to ignore my true nature and pretend to be something else. But I didn't even know how to begin to explain that to her, so I said, "Because I love him. More than anyone or anything in the world." I wrapped my left hand around his. "Because Ival is my husband, and I honestly don't care if you find the very idea blasphemous. I swore vows before God I consider sacred, and if the rest of the world doesn't understand, the fault is in them."

"But—"

"No." I was done with this. Done with arguing; done with defending myself. "You talk about the parson and the men of Sodom, but God doesn't hate me. God made me this way, and I don't care what anyone else says." I stroked a lock of Ival's hair back from his forehead; predictably, it immediately sprang forward again. "God didn't make you torment a man who didn't deserve it, who already had enough pain in his life. Didn't make the newspapers print insinuations about him, or the ladies of the town refuse to socialize with his wife, or any of it. You chose that yourselves, you and the rest of Fallow."

"Griffin…" she trailed off.

"I love you, Ma, and I'll always be grateful you took me in as a boy. But right now, I need you to go." I leaned forward, pressed my forehead against Whyborne's arm. "Keep an eye on Creigh if you like, and shout if she does anything suspicious. But at the moment, my husband is my only concern. I hope you can understand that."

CHAPTER 31

Whyborne

I OPENED MY eyes and found myself lying on an uncomfortable bed, in a strange room. Sunlight streamed through a dirty window, illuminating a million motes of dust floating slowly through the air. There seemed to be no blankets on the bed, as there were no curtains on the window, but Griffin's coat lay over me.

My head pounded, and my mouth tasted like ash. Where was I? How had I gotten here? I cast my memory back, trying to bridge the gap. Vernon at the farm…Griffin bound to a scarecrow…hands gripping me as foul water was forced down my throat…

Then rage. And magic.

Oh God.

I sat up sharply. "Griffin?"

He'd been sitting propped against the wall, perhaps dozing. His head jerked up at the sound of my voice, however, and his eyes widened. An ugly bruise decorated his jaw, and dried blood crusted in his hair, but he moved quickly to my side.

"Ival?" He caught my hands in his, his eyes searching my face desperately. "How are you feeling, my dear?"

I swallowed; the sides of my throat felt as though they stuck together. "Thirsty."

"Here." He splashed water out of a canteen into a tin cup, then passed it to me.

I drank greedily, washing the taste of ash from my mouth. "Where are we?" I asked, passing the cup back to him for more.

He didn't answer until he'd refilled the cup for me. "Inside the abandoned jewelry store. We thought it would be the most secure place to hide, with the best locks on the doors and windows. I don't know if you recall the wagon ride…?"

I shook my head.

"I'd be surprised if you did. To make a long and frightening story short, we took Tate's wagon and fled. Marian is in control of the entire town, after providing corrupted food for the community dance. Creigh apparently decided throwing in with us was the only way to save her skin; she's currently downstairs, under guard by Christine and Ma."

Oh God, poor Christine. "Iskander?"

Griffin looked away. "We had to leave him behind. After we brought you here, Christine drove the horses and cart to the Reynolds farm, warned them to leave, and gave them the wagon to take with them. Once she came back, I ransacked the general store for supplies, and we took refuge here before dawn."

"I see." I pressed my fingers into my aching eyes. "Won't the theft at the general store arouse suspicion?"

"Ordinarily." The grim note in his voice made me drop my hands and look at him again. "Except the town is deserted. I think Marian has everyone occupied with bringing in the last of the harvest to be loaded into the train cars."

"She means to continue Creigh's plan, then?"

"Or a version of it." Griffin shook his head. "We think she wants to go to Widdershins and feed directly on the maelstrom. With its power, there's no limit to how many infected she might create. Might control."

"Dear God." How were we to fight her? We had to stop her somehow, had to rescue Iskander and find some way of removing the corruption from him.

Griffin moved to sit beside me on the bed. "Ival?" he said softly. "You don't recall the wagon ride, but what about before? In the field?"

I shrank into myself. The things I'd said, while the power of the arcane line sang through me...I'd sounded like some sort of cheap stage villain. "What do you mean?" I asked in one last, feeble attempt to stave off the inevitable.

"You were able to-to burn away the corruption from yourself, and in the reservoir beneath the earth," he said. "By drawing on the arcane line."

"Yes." I stared down at my hands, at the lacework of scars covering the right. "The rust is a parasite. It feeds on arcane energy. But only in measured doses."

"The way a man needs water to survive, but can still drown in a lake?" Griffin asked. "Or a campfire can keep you alive in the cold, but being set on fire will kill you?"

"Something like that," I agreed.

"And when you burned away the corruption," he went on, "you said...things. You seemed not entirely yourself."

I wished that were true. The problem was I'd been entirely myself. I'd *felt* the rest of the maelstrom, distantly, through the line.

Had Persephone sensed my anger last night? Some unexplained flash of rage, that this crawling parasite would dare attack us?

"Do you remember the day of Christine's wedding?" I kept my gaze fixed on my hands, because I couldn't bear to look at his face. "When I asked if you thought me human at all?"

Out of the corner of my eye, I saw him nod. "Yes. I said after the things we've seen, that it didn't matter."

"You were wrong," I said. My heart ached, but I owed him the truth. "It matters a great deal."

I confessed everything: what I'd experienced that night. The confirmation that the maelstrom did indeed collect people.

That it had collected him.

And that Persephone and I were a part of it, fragments of the maelstrom's inhuman sentience, given form. It wasn't a matter of us being human or even ketoi.

We weren't even people at all.

When I finished, Griffin's hand closed on mine. "Ival...I saw you." He sounded strangely awed, when he should have been horrified. "In that moment after Bradley's body crumbled, and yours was lying stabbed through the heart. I *saw* you. And I didn't understand at the time why my shadowsight would reveal such a thing…but it makes sense." He laughed, a short sound of amazement. "I once said you *are* magic. I was far more right than I realized."

How could he not understand? "Griffin, listen to me! This isn't something—something wonderful."

I looked at him at last, only to find him smiling at me. "I disagree," he said simply.

I'd failed to explain. In my cowardice, I hadn't shown him clearly enough the wreck I'd made of his life. "Listen to me," I repeated. "You encountered the umbra in Chicago, and it changed you."

"Which was in no way your fault," he pointed out.

Why did he insist on focusing on the wrong details? "But that… that should have been the end of it! No more magic. No more horror. After you left here, you should have gone somewhere safe. Somewhere that made sense for a man starting his own private detective business. Boston, or New York, or Baltimore…but you didn't."

Griffin swallowed. At least he wasn't smiling any more. "The arcane line in the fields. The same one the rust fed on. The maelstrom…sensed…me through it?"

At last he seemed to understand. "Yes, but it's worse than that." I bowed my head, because I couldn't bear to see his reaction when he realized this final truth. "Even then…you might have gone free. You weren't the only person within the maelstrom's reach who had been touched by an umbra or some other monstrous thing. There were others it might have collected." I took a deep breath, fighting to keep my voice steady. "But it didn't. It chose you. I think it knew, somehow, that you'd—you'd *see* me. See past the walls I'd built around my life, my heart."

I buried my face in my hands in despair. "You should never have been involved in any of this," I confessed. "All the fear of the last few years, all the narrow escapes, all the pain and horror…you wouldn't have suffered any of it if not for me. It's all my fault, and I can only pray you don't hate me."

CHAPTER 32

Griffin

I SAT BESIDE Ival on the bed, holding myself very still, while his words sunk in.

Years ago, when Miss Lester first suggested to me that Widdershins collected people, I'd dismissed her words. Over time, though, I'd come to believe her correct. Something had drawn me to my Ival's side; God's will, perhaps, or divine providence.

And maybe that was indeed the ultimate truth. Surely a semi-sentient magical vortex could fit into God's plan. But all my hopes for God's will were abstract, pure faith, whereas this…this was something solid. Something I could hold onto as a fact.

The maelstrom had chosen me.

I remembered with searing clarity how broken I'd been when Pa brought me back to Fallow. Even when I'd left again, the pieces of myself had felt held together with spackling paste and cheap glue.

I'd been at my very worst. My lowest point; hurt and fractured, my nights shattered by terrifying fits. Wounded, body and soul.

And *that* was when it chose me. Because in whatever inhuman way the maelstrom perceived the world, it saw worth in me even then. Even when no one else had.

Even when I hadn't seen it in myself.

Ma had needed to blame Benjamin so she could keep loving me. If she admitted the truth to herself, it meant I wasn't the son she'd believed me to be. That I was imperfect. But Widdershins didn't care about perfection. Widdershins knew its own.

And maybe that was the real secret: its own were the flawed, the broken, the wounded. But they—we—I—had value even so.

My eyes burned, and I blinked rapidly. "Thank you," I whispered.

Ival looked at me as if I'd lost my mind. "What?"

I didn't know how I could adequately explain what it meant to me. "Maybe it chose me because I could see you, but it had to see me first." I swallowed against the thickness in my throat. "It saw me, and it chose me, and it brought me home."

He frowned slightly. "It didn't bring you to Fallow, Griffin."

"Home. Widdershins." I took his hands, and he didn't pull away. "You." I met his gaze, let all the raw emotion that I could express show. "Don't you understand? Ma and Pa chose me from the orphan train, but when I proved to be less than perfect, they sent me away. I spent most of my life trying to earn my place, trying to deserve it. To be worthy of choosing. The perfect son, the perfect friend, the perfect detective. And I failed."

"Griffin, no," he said alarmed.

"Hush. Let me finish." I brought his hands to my lips and kissed them. "I failed Pa when I couldn't make myself stop wanting men, and he put me on a train to Chicago. I failed Elliot and the Pinkertons when I screamed about monsters, and they put me in an asylum and forgot about me." I drew his hands against my chest, over my heart. "You said the maelstrom might have taken others, but I was the one it chose. It wanted *me*, for who I was. And that means everything to me."

Ival blinked rapidly. "But…if you'd just gone to Boston instead…"

"I'd be safer? Perhaps. But I wouldn't have found my home. I wouldn't have found you." I stared into his dark eyes, trying to make him understand by force of will. "Perhaps Widdershins needed me for its inscrutable purposes, but I needed it, too."

He looked flummoxed. "But…it's a horrible murder town!"

I couldn't help but laugh. "Well, I'm sure no enormous magical vortex is perfect, my dear."

"You're…" he trailed off, apparently unable to decide precisely what I was. "I thought you'd be hurt, or angry, or…I don't know." He shook his head. "I don't always understand you. But I love you, Griffin. I'd do anything in the world just to make you happy."

"You do make me happy, Ival. I love you, too." I tugged him into my arms, and our lips met.

I'd meant the kiss to be gentle, but he responded with desperate passion. How long had this weighed on his mind? At least now I understood the mood that had gripped him since July, his desperate attempts to take every responsibility on his own shoulders. How could he have possibly imagined I'd be angry? That I'd hate him? My own husband?

"I'm yours," I whispered in his ear. "And you're mine. Nothing in this world can ever change that."

His hands gripped my vest. "Show me."

I glanced at the window. The sun was high—too high to dare sneaking out of the jewelry store, certainly for hours to come. There was time.

I freed myself from his embrace just long enough to ease the bedroom door closed, in case anyone decided to come check on us. He stripped off his clothing as I did so, then attacked mine once I rejoined him.

The bed was uncomfortable, and we were both filthy from sweat and dust, but I didn't care. I pulled him close, kissing and nipping at his neck, until he squirmed against me. I stroked the scars lacing his right arm, then made my way down, mapping his chest and belly with my mouth. He tasted of salt and dry earth, but he smelled like the ocean.

I lavished attention on his cock and balls, sucking and licking without haste. His fingers threaded into my hair, tightening as I traced the veins on his prick with my tongue. "Griffin," he whispered. "Please hold me. I need to see your face."

I paused just long enough to lap at his slit before obeying. He caught me fiercely to him, kissing me hard. I wrapped my arms around him tight, and flung a leg over his hip. "I see you," I murmured, once he let me speak again. "And I love what I see. More than I would ever have thought possible."

He slipped a hand between us, gripping first his cock, then curling his long fingers around mine as well. I kissed him, lips parted, and then sucked hard on his tongue when he slipped it into my mouth. A shudder went through him, hips bucking, rubbing our bodies together. I loved the feel of him against me; I loved his scent and his taste, the way he laughed, the line between his brows when he concentrated, everything.

He pulled his mouth free of mine, back arching—then bit me on the shoulder to muffle a cry. Hot semen coated my belly and cock, and the sting of his teeth sent a jolt through me. I swallowed back a shout and lost myself to the pleasure of it all, until we were both slick with our mutual spend.

My coat was ruined anyway, so I used it to clean us up as best I could, then hurled it into a corner. Whyborne curled up against me, his head on my shoulder. I kissed his brow and wrapped my arm around his shoulders.

As I stared at the unfamiliar ceiling, a sharp, almost painful longing for our own bed in our own house gripped me. I'd always told myself it didn't matter where I lay my head, but that wasn't true anymore.

It hadn't been for a long time now.

"I belong in Widdershins," I said quietly. "And I will fight with everything in me to save it."

His lips pressed against my shoulder, over the mark where he'd bitten me in his passion. "Then we should probably move, as much as I would prefer to stay here." He sat up, then frowned. "Wait. Did you say your mother is downstairs?"

~ * ~

Christine looked up when Whyborne and I emerged onto the lower floor. She sat near the door, pistol in her hand, the rifle I'd scavenged from the general store across her lap. Their eyes met; neither of them said anything, but Whyborne opened his arms.

They held each other for a while in silence. Eventually, he drew back and kissed her forehead. "We're going to save him."

"I know that," she muttered, and punched Whyborne on the arm.

"Ow." He glared at her, rubbing his arm. "There's something I have to tell you. About last night." He glanced pointedly at Creigh. "Privately."

"We don't have time for this," Creigh said. "We need to plan."

"The backroom should do," I said, and led the way past the empty counters. Christine picked up a burlap sack and followed us back.

The room was tiny and windowless, occupied only by a large safe which must have once held the more valuable pieces. Christine shut the door, then opened the sack. "I made sure to bring this back from the farm with me," she said, pulling out the bottle of whiskey the porter had given her on the train. "I rather thought we might need it."

We passed the bottle around. Keeping his voice low, Whyborne explained to Christine everything he'd told me about the maelstrom.

"I love you, Whyborne," Christine said when he'd finished. "But you're an idiot."

He glared at her. "Thank you, Christine. I'm so glad Widdershins collected you."

A slight frown crossed her face. "But what about K-Kander?" Her eyes glistened slightly, but no tears fell. "He came to Widdershins to be with me. Didn't he?"

"Of course he did. The maelstrom doesn't alter people's emotions," Whyborne said. "Just...probabilities, you might say. But changing anyone would defeat the purpose. It might have made certain your paths crossed, but possibly not even that."

"Well, I do understand it wanting the best archaeologist," Christine said with a firm nod. "And if it brought Kander to me, even better."

Whyborne shook his head and took a pull from the bottle. "Don't any of you recall it's a horrible murder town?"

"I don't give a fig, if its influence got me into the field," Christine replied. "It needed us, but we needed it, too. I don't see why you're complaining because we're happy with our lives. Although I must say all of this sorcery nonsense has interfered with my career over the last few years." Then she brightened. "Which means you owe it to me to come to Egypt and clear the fane of deadly magic so I can do a proper excavation."

"Perhaps we should concentrate on saving Iskander and surviving this first," I said. "Hopefully Creigh will have the answers we need."

"She said if we kill Marian, the rust will go dormant," Christine said. "The corrupted will be freed, and in time their bodies will clear it as any infection. Except for the cinereous, of course; they're too far gone." She gave us a quizzical look. "Surely you don't believe I was simply sitting and moping down here while Whyborne was taking his nap."

"Never," I said. "So I take it you have a plan, then?"

"Yes. It involves my rifle, a bullet, and Marian's head."

"Simple and straightforward." I saluted her with the bottle. "I approve."

"I still want to talk to Creigh," Whyborne said.

We returned to the main room. Before we could say anything, Creigh snapped, "Are you finished? Can we get to the important matter of not dying at Marian's hands now?"

Whyborne folded his arms over his chest, using his full height to glare down at Creigh. "Tell us what you had planned here, from the beginning." When she hesitated, he gestured at the window. "Whatever plan you had is in ruins. The reservoir of rust spores beneath the ground has been destroyed. Marian has slipped the leash, and given that she can eat any spell you try to cast on her, I can't imagine you'll be able to get her back under control. You've lost."

"And whose fault is that?" Creigh demanded.

"Oh, yes, we should have just let you kill us all," Christine said with a roll of her eyes. "What terrible inconvenience we've caused you."

"How were you able to cast the spell in the first place?" I asked Creigh. "If the corrupted feed on magic."

"Only the avatar can directly absorb spells, not all of the corrupted. And because she consented to it." Creigh sighed, as though our questions were an annoying distraction. "Very well. The Fideles have long scoured the earth, looking for old works of the masters. Not umbrae or ketoi—we don't wish to be seen as consorting with rebels, after all. Fallow was one of the locations we suspected might harbor something unusual."

"Because of the barren spot?" I guessed.

She nodded. "Yes. A bit of research into certain arcane volumes, and we even suspected what it might be." She offered a cold smile to Whyborne. "You don't have the key to the Wisborg Codex, do you?"

Whyborne scowled. "Go on."

"If you did, you'd have recognized the import of the transferal sphere. Delancey probably took it with him under the assumption you'd know what it was. Did he live long enough to be disappointed?"

"Just tell us what the damned thing is," Christine growled. "It had something to do with the corruption, obviously."

"During the time of the masters, it—and others like it—were used to seed the rust spores from place to place." Creigh folded her arms over her chest and leaned back slightly, as though she enjoyed lecturing us. "Some acolyte must have brought it here to hide when they left this world for the Outside. Eons it lay beneath the earth. Over time, the corruption did as it was meant, and...hatched isn't quite the right word, I suppose. Burned its way out of its artificial shell.

"We thought the fallow place might mark such an event, but we weren't sure. So we came here and set about drilling. Luckily for me, there was not only a drought, but one of the landowners whose farm bordered the fallow place was...amenable to certain suggestions." She glanced at me. "Your cousin Vernon—but he isn't really your cousin, is he?"

"That's none of your concern," Whyborne said, and his breath frosted the air.

"He'd come here to prove himself, but his farm was failing," Creigh went on. "It didn't take much to see either the ambition burning in him, or the rage in his wife. Oh, how she longed for her revenge against this wretched town." She turned to Ma, who'd been sitting quietly in the corner ever since Whyborne and I came downstairs. "I take it I have you to thank for that."

"Leave her out of this," I said sharply.

Creigh shrugged. "As you wish. We found the transferal sphere, which both confirmed what we suspected and told us where we needed to put the main well. So I offered Marian and Vernon both what they wanted most. Vernon would prosper when all others failed. Marian would see at least some members of the community suffer. The fact I offered to form her into the instrument controlling them made it impossible to refuse."

"That's it," Whyborne said suddenly. The rest of us looked at him in surprise. "The pattern."

"What are you going on about?" Christine asked.

"There's a pattern to the masters' creations," he said, voice rising in excitement. "The god commands the ketoi—or at least speaks to them. Presumably before the rebellion, the masters would somehow give orders to the god, and it would pass those along to the ketoi. The umbrae are a more refined version, you might say. The Mother of Shadows takes the place of the god in the hierarchy, and all her children follow her commands due their very biology. The rust's control—"

"The avatar," Creigh put in. "The first infected."

"The avatar controls the others corrupted by the rust." He paled. "And the maelstrom reaches out and influences those it finds valuable…"

I put my hand to his arm, squeezing tight. "What did you just say, about the maelstrom not influencing the way those it chooses think and feel, because that would defeat the purpose?" I asked. "That sounds the precise opposite of the rust."

"Quite right," Christine said.

Creigh looked at Whyborne speculatively. "What are you?" she murmured.

"Once again, that's none of your concern," I snapped.

Whyborne put his hand on mine briefly, then let it fall. "In the case of both the Mother of Shadows and the avatar, the masters used an enchanted gem to compel them to obey. I wonder if they had something similar for the dweller in the deeps?" He frowned. "Where did you come upon the enchanted jewel you used to command the avatar?"

She glanced at me. "That's none of your concern."

"As fascinating as this is, it's academic at the moment," I said. "Go on, Creigh. You infected Marian, then your charges at the poor farm. You convinced the mayor's family to join in your little scheme, giving you even more of a grip on the community. You sent Odell and Evers to Widdershins."

"To keep an eye on things for us there, yes. Not that they realized Marian was watching through them. At least, until we needed to control their actions directly."

"Because you meant to infect Widdershins, just as Marian infected Fallow." A slow rage built in me at the thought, and I took a deep breath for calm.

"Of course." Creigh shrugged. "Why wouldn't we? Widdershins isn't *just* a source of immense power currently lost to us—it's where the masters will return from the Outside. If they emerge through the veil into the middle of a town set against them, it won't look as if we've done a proper job, now will it? Two birds with one stone—we'd get access to the maelstrom's power, and secure Widdershins for the masters." Her eyes narrowed. "If Delancey's nerve hadn't failed…but it did."

"You knew—or guessed—he was coming to Widdershins," Whyborne said. "And you ordered Odell to stop him."

"Yes. Another failure—Odell was slow and didn't locate him until too late. You were warned."

"Why have them harangue and try to kill Griffin?" Christine asked. "We would have investigated anyway, but it certainly lent the situation some urgency."

Creigh straightened, her pale brows drawing down. "What?"

"That was all Marian," I said. "From the beginning. She blamed me for Benjamin's death, or at least the events leading up to it. She wanted me to pay for what I'd done."

Christine gave Creigh a nasty smile. "It looks like she was slipping the leash from the start. Vernon was right—you shouldn't have underestimated her."

"Indeed." Creigh's eyes snapped with angry fire. "I thought it would be easier to keep her in line if I offered her a bit of leeway. I should have known better than to treat a tool as an equal. It isn't a mistake I'll make again."

"Yes, that's certainly the lesson we should all take from this," Christine muttered.

Whyborne and I exchanged a glance. What we would do with Creigh once our very temporary alliance was over, I didn't know. Certainly we couldn't with good conscience unleash her back on the world.

But that was a worry for later. For now, we needed to get close enough to Marian to kill her, without coming to a bad end ourselves. "All right," I began.

I got no farther. The sound of a train whistle cut through the still air, coming from the direction of the grain elevator spur.

Whyborne's eyes went wide. "Oh no. They must almost be ready to move the grain, if they've the engine running and steam built up."

Christine had stepped to the window at the sound. "Damn it. We have a problem."

I joined her at the window. A large group of townsfolk shuffled down the center of the street. Their faces were slack, and they moved in eerie formation as they made their way directly toward us.

CHAPTER 33

Whyborne

THE STEAM WHISTLE sounded again, its distant scream drawing my nerves tight. The train was like a dagger, aimed right at the heart of Widdershins.

We couldn't let it arrive. But Marian didn't mean to make it easy on us.

How she'd discovered us, I couldn't guess. Most likely, one of the corrupted townsfolk had noticed some clue as to where we'd gone.

I stared out the window at them. The setting sun lowered onto the horizon, painting their features in amber light. "I don't see Kander," Christine said, and though her tone was calm, I heard the fear beneath the words.

I put a hand to her shoulder. "There's Miss Tate. Still wearing her dress from the community dance. I owe her an apology—it might have seen Fifth Avenue after all."

"Can we talk to them?" Nella asked. "I know them—they'll listen to me."

I didn't look at her. While we dressed after making love, Griffin had told me what she'd done. Between her letters, the blasted editor of the newspaper, and people like Mr. Tate, Benjamin's life must have been hell. No wonder Marian wanted everyone dead.

"They're under the influence of magic, Ma," Griffin said. "You can't reason with them."

"No," I said. "But we can use them."

Christine glanced at me. "You have a plan?"

"The livery stable is down the street. I'll delay them while you secure a cart." I glanced at Creigh. "You said Marian can see through their eyes. So we make absolutely certain they see us leaving town in the cart. Especially Nella."

Griffin frowned. "Whyborne…"

"The rest of us abandon the cart and circle back around, the first opportunity we have." I turned to face Nella. "You keep driving, but not so fast as for them to lose your trail. Animals hate them, so they'll have to go on foot after you. Pretend there's a problem with one of the horses, the cart, I don't care, but make sure they stay on your trail. Marian won't pass up the opportunity to kill you. It will keep both us and the infected townspeople safe."

"Some of them are armed!" Griffin exclaimed hotly. "You're putting my mother in danger!"

Nella met my gaze. "I'll do it," she said to me. "If you promise not to let anything happen to my boy."

"I don't owe you anything." I glared down at her. "What you did to Benjamin Walter was heinous. Griffin knows I would die for him, and that's all that matters. I don't give a damn for your opinion."

"There's no time for this," Creigh snapped.

Nella didn't look at all happy, but she nodded. "All right. I'll do it."

"Then let's hurry," Christine said.

"Indeed." I went to the door. "Go out the back way. I'll distract them."

"Be careful, Ival," Griffin called after me.

The eyes of the corrupted fixed on me the moment I stepped into the street. My charred shirt sleeve fluttered in the wind, and I set myself squarely in their path. Waiting.

Parson Norton was at the forefront. He'd refused to let Benjamin Walter be buried in the church yard, inflicting one more cruelty on Marian in the midst of her grief. Was the newspaper editor Carson among them as well? The one who'd run Vernon's slander, naming Griffin a lunatic, insinuating there was something unnatural about Christine and Iskander's marriage.

How many of these men and women would turn on us given half the chance?

God, I understood Marian's rage, all too well. No wonder she wanted to see her fellow townsfolk brought low. If our positions were reversed, if I lost Griffin the way she lost Benjamin, I wouldn't have left a single house in Fallow standing.

They were running now. Coming for me in a group, with enough numbers to overwhelm if I let them reach me. And maybe there was something of savage satisfaction in me, when I reached into the sky and called down the wind

It howled like an unleashed animal. The blast ripped down the street, tearing a sign loose from a storefront. The sign flew through the air, striking one of the men on the arm. He cried out, and several of the corrupted staggered under the force of the gale.

In the hands of the wind, the desiccated earth rose in a cloud of dust. Within moments, it transformed into a wall of brown, a sandstorm that blotted out all visibility only a few feet from me. I glimpsed the corrupted flinging up their arms, trying to protect their eyes and still stagger closer, but the stinging dust storm kept them back

I wanted to do more than keep them back. I wanted to hurt them.

But Griffin would only remind me some of them might be innocent of any wrongdoing. Miss Tate was among them, just as the Reynolds could have easily been, had we not warned them away from the community dance.

"Whyborne!" Griffin shouted from behind me.

I let the wind go. The dust hung in the air, a loose cloud that began to slowly settle to earth.

Nella drove a cart drawn by two horses into the street, Griffin, Creigh, and Christine all piled into the back. I ran to join them, and Griffin and Christine pulled me into the moving cart.

I glanced back, saw the corrupted regrouping. They were coated in dust, and many wiped at their eyes, but Marian clearly didn't intend for us to get away so easily.

Griffin's hand rested on my shoulder. "Well done, my dear."

I put my hand over his as the cart raced out of town, down the unnaturally straight road. At least the utter flatness of the landscape would keep it in sight of the corrupted longer, once we abandoned it. With luck, they wouldn't realize Nella was alone until we'd dealt with Marian.

"Thank you," I said. "Now comes the difficult part. We have to kill Marian, but we also need to make certain the train doesn't leave town." I turned to Creigh. "Mrs. Creigh, I have a proposition for you."

~ * ~

Night had fallen by the time we reached the grain elevators.

Our plan, such as it had been, seemed to have worked. After hiding in a barn while the group of corrupted followed Nella farther and farther out of Fallow, we'd slipped back into town as the sun slid below the horizon. Christine had sought out a vantage point from which to fire on Marian, assuming she was at the grain elevators with her minions. Griffin went with her, while Creigh and I made our way to the elevators and the train spur.

The glow of lanterns painted the scene in ruddy red, and the train's headlight cast its beam down the spur toward the main line. The scents of hot iron and burning coal filled the air, mingled with dust and tons of corn. The whistle screamed again, making me jump.

Dozens of people milled around the train and elevators. Most of the town must have been involved in bringing in the final bits of harvest and then filling the boxcars. In addition, a large group of cinereous lurked along the track, clearly keeping watch.

Blast.

"We should set the grain elevators on fire," Creigh suggested. The two of us crouched in the shadow of the freight office. "They're probably full of grain dust right now. Apply the right spark, and they'll go up as if they were filled with dynamite."

"No," I said. I could see smaller figures moving in the lantern light, though I couldn't make out their faces at a distance. "There are children amongst the elevators. Innocents. If we set off a grain dust explosion, we'll kill them along with the cinereous." Not to mention Iskander. I hadn't seen him yet, but he must be here somewhere.

Creigh let out an impatient hiss of disgust. "This is precisely why you'll lose to the masters. You're not willing to make the necessary sacrifices."

We didn't have time to argue. "I need to get to the front of the train," I murmured. "If we can sabotage the engine, we can insure all the grain stays here in Fallow. Then we can worry about destroying it."

A jumble of carts and wagons stood all around the elevators and train spur. Presumably they'd brought the last of the corrupted harvest to the elevators, then been abandoned. We slipped from shadow to shadow, careful to keep the wagons between us and the light. Trembling horses and mules stood between the traces of some, their eyes showing white. Other wagons appeared to have been dragged here using manpower alone.

The door on the final boxcar slammed shut. "All aboard!" Vernon called.

All but holding my breath, I crouched down and peered beneath the wagon we currently hid behind. The gravel of the rail bed crunched as Vernon made his way to the caboose. A bandage swathed his head, concealing the wound Creigh had dealt him in the field. "Next stop: Widdershins."

"I can't wait," Marian said, stepping around from the far side of the train and into view.

My knees turned to water at the sight of her. Creigh's spell must have somehow kept the corruption in check, because in less than a day it had transformed her utterly. But not into a gray-skinned horror, but something else. Something almost as beautiful as it was revolting.

The nubs on her forehead had sprouted, turning into fungal spikes reminiscent of the horns of a stag. Her skin had taken on a sickly white smoothness. A sort of lacy, veil-like growth fell delicately from her forehead, over her eyes, then fused again with her cheeks. Her clothing was replaced with layers of growth reminiscent of bracket mushrooms, encircling her as stiff as the skirts of half a century past. Clusters of growths like fat tentacles erupted from each shoulder in some parody of wings, their orange color shocking against the whiteness of her rubbery flesh.

There came the crack of a rifle, and Marian's head burst apart.

CHAPTER 34

Griffin

CHRISTINE AND I stole two more horses from the livery stable, tying them up on the far side of the building whose roof she'd chosen as a perch. Few structures in Fallow were more than a story tall, and we were able to scramble onto the tin roof with the help of a convenient telegraph pole.

The darkness of the night meant we'd likely go unseen—but it also meant we dared use no light ourselves, without giving away our location. We crawled on our bellies across the roof, until we could peer over the edge and see the railroad spur and train.

"Will this do?" I whispered to Christine.

"It will have to." She settled in, sighting through her rifle, her finger resting just behind the trigger. "Now where is Marian?"

I squinted at the figures of the cinereous lined watchfully along the track. Whyborne would somehow have to get past them to reach the train. "Do you see Iskander anywhere?"

"No. Nor Marian."

Vernon appeared, walking up the track toward the caboose. Even at this distance, I could make out the triumphant grin on his face.

"Should I try for Vernon?" Christine asked. "That would draw Marian out, I'm guessing."

I half wanted to say yes. But if she fired now, she'd give away our position. If she didn't get a clear shot at Marian before the cinereous found us, we'd be in desperate trouble. "No," I said. "Wait for Marian. She's too much of a threat to waste what might be our only chance."

We didn't wait long.

The sight of the horror Marian had become turned my stomach. Christine cursed softly in Arabic—then fired.

The bullet punched directly through Marian's head, scattering chunks of something spongey and curiously homogenous, like the interior of a mushroom. She staggered from the impact.

But she didn't fall.

"Marian!" cried Vernon, and started to run to her. Then stopped when she raised a hand.

Marian straightened slowly. The hole in the side of her head where the bullet had entered sealed, and the rest began to grow back at a frightening rate.

"Oh, for God's sake," Christine said, lowering the rifle. "I hope we have another plan."

Marian's antler-crowned head swiveled in our direction. "Destroy them," she ordered. Then she turned back to Vernon. "Get on the train. It's time to go to our new home."

Even as she spoke, the train let out a blast of steam and began to grind into motion. Marian strode toward the front of the train, while Vernon climbed onto the caboose.

And the cinereous began to move en masse in our direction.

CHAPTER 35

Whyborne

"Oh, of all the damnable luck," Creigh said.

I stared in horror at the white chunks lying on the ground, which had been a part of Marian's head. She'd healed so quickly—and she hadn't even fallen when the bullet spread her head everywhere.

How in the world were we to kill her?

The train lurched into motion. Smoke belched from the stack, and the whistle howled into the night.

The cinereous were moving now, with purpose. The lantern light gleamed off the slick, sickly gray of their skins. The stench of mildew now fought with the stink of the train. They'd be on us at any moment, and our flimsy hiding spot would be discovered.

Everything was going wrong. I was nowhere near the head of the train, and though it was moving slowly now, it would soon overcome the inertia of tons of corn and reach a speed I couldn't hope to match.

"We need to get to the train!" I said. "Before it leaves us behind!"

"If we'd set fire to the elevators as I suggested," Creigh began.

"No," I said. "Not fire. Ice. Can you cast a spell in tandem with me?"

She looked startled—then nodded. "Yes."

I rose to my feet and stepped out from behind the cart. The nearest of the cinereous immediately shifted their attention to me.

Good.

Creigh followed me. "Now," she said, and began to chant.

I didn't take her hand, as I had Persephone's when we'd cast a spell together. But I joined my voice to Creigh's. Even though I didn't need to speak the Aklo words, I hoped doing so would more completely blend our power.

I felt the world stir. The temperature around us plummeted, and frost began to spread over the ground. My body hummed like a tuning fork, my voice modulating and harmonizing with Creigh's.

The fingers of the cinereous brushed against me, just as our chant reached its crescendo.

Cold snapped out from us, and the cinereous froze in place. Quite literally.

Creigh slumped, gasping—the spell had taken a great deal from her, it seemed. But then she laughed, reached out, and snapped off the crumbling hand of the nearest cinereous. "Well done, Dr. Whyborne."

The train whistle screamed.

Her eyes widened. "Go!" she barked. The few remaining cinereous were coming up on us now, and she turned to face them. "I'll hold them off. Get on the train. If Marian reaches Widdershins and feeds on the vortex, we're all doomed."

I broke and ran for the train, even as the last of the cinereous descended on her. The train rapidly picked up speed, so I put my head down and raced alongside as fast as I could. Boxcars rolled past, faster and faster, and I caught a glimpse of the caboose coming up behind me. Within moments, it would be alongside, and I'd either miss the train altogether or find myself fighting Vernon.

I leapt for the rungs welded to the side of the last boxcar.

One hand closed securely on the iron rung—but the fingers of the other slipped, and neither foot found purchase. For a terrifying moment, I swung free. The rail ties flashed past beneath my dangling feet. The iron wheels would surely crush me if I fell beneath them.

Then my scrabbling fingers found purchase, taking some of the strain from my shoulder. A moment later, my feet rested on the lowest rung. I clung to the side of the boxcar, my face pressed against the metal, my lungs gasping for breath.

I couldn't waste time. I needed to move, before someone realized I'd boarded the train.

Once my limbs had stopped trembling too badly, I pulled myself up the ladder to the roof of the boxcar. The wind caught my hair and screamed past my ears. Swallowing hard, I scrambled across the roof and stared at the gap to the next car.

Then I lifted my gaze. There were a great many cars between me and the engine.

I looked back at the gap. It wasn't that big, surely. Men working on the trains made the jump with ease all the time.

Gathering the rags of my courage, I backed up a few steps, then dashed forward and leapt.

CHAPTER 36

Griffin

CHRISTINE AND I scrambled off the roof and to the ground. The horses we'd stolen from the livery stable were already tossing their heads and blowing at the smell of rot on the dry wind. We mounted with difficulty, and I firmed my hold on the reins. Hopefully the skills I'd honed while chasing down train robbers in the west were still with me.

Our horses began to balk even before we came in sight of the corrupted. I tightened my grip with my knees, and urged my mount forward. In one hand I held the reins, and in the other the revolver I'd taken from the general store.

Then we came around the side of the depot, and I gaped at what I saw. A great patch of frost coated the ground in a circle around Creigh. Some of the cinereous stood, literally frozen, their damaged bodies crumbling and flaking as they began to thaw.

But others made their way toward her still. I fired, but the bullet only slammed into the shoulder of one. My second shot took it through the head, and it fell.

Then my horse let out a whinny of fear, half-rearing in its desperation to get away from them. I tightened my grip on the reins. "Where is Whyborne?" I shouted.

"On the train!" Creigh said. "Go! While you can still catch up! I'll hold them off."

Christine tossed her pistol to Creigh, who caught it with a nod. We wheeled our horses, circling around the cinereous, before giving the frightened beasts their head. As they plunged up the track, I heard shots ring out behind us.

I leaned in close to my steed's mane as we pounded alongside the rails, the train picking up speed even as we did. The lights of the caboose drew slowly nearer, but it wouldn't be long before the train outpaced the horses.

I urged my mount faster. It put on a final burst of speed, bringing me even with the caboose. I grabbed the rail, said a prayer, and swung from horse to platform.

The door opened, and Vernon stepped out, an ax in his hand.

I ducked, and the blade of the ax bit into the railing inches from me. As he lifted it again, I brought my knee up, but my aim was off and I made contact with his thigh instead of his crotch. Even so, he grunted and staggered slightly.

A bullet from Christine's rifle buried itself in the side of the caboose. Vernon jumped, and I took the opportunity to slam my fist into his stomach. As he doubled over, I seized hold of the haft of the ax, just above where he held it. We struggled for possession—then he lurched suddenly forward, shoving the ax and himself at me.

My back struck the railing, and only my grip on the ax kept me from toppling over and onto the tracks. Vernon grinned and pinned me against it, the ax handle pressing against my neck now.

"You should have stayed in Widdershins," he growled. The rail dug into my back, and the muscles of my arms shook as I strove to keep the handle from my windpipe. "No—you should've stayed in New York, died there with your real family, and left us decent folk alone."

Christine swung onto the platform and kicked Vernon in the knee.

He staggered to the side, and I surged forward, off the rail. Letting go of the ax, I drew my revolver. "Vernon, stop, or—"

He raised the ax, prefatory to splitting my head like a block of wood.

I fired.

The ax fell from his hands onto the platform. For a moment, he stared at me aghast. Then he collapsed slowly backward, over the side of the platform. I looked back and glimpsed his motionless body lying on the tracks, before the train left him behind.

"Good riddance," Christine said.

I put away my revolver and picked up the ax. "We have to get to the front of the train," I said. "That's where Marian will be."

Christine nodded. I tucked the ax through my belt, grasped the ladder leading to the roof of the caboose, and began to climb.

CHAPTER 37

Whyborne

I WAS DOING surprisingly well at leaping from one car to the next, in that I'd cleared half the train and not yet fallen to my death.

The train hurtled into the night, moving far faster than the eighteen miles per hour freight locomotives were supposed to restrict themselves to. Then again, even human engineers tended to ignore the limit; I shouldn't have been surprised Marian chose to do so as well.

The wind tore at my hair as I crossed yet another boxcar. When I reached the gap, I paused, crouching at the edge. I couldn't let myself think about how fast we were moving, or what would happen if I misjudged and fell between the cars. I just had to keep going.

I pulled my hand back, and a knife slammed into the metal precisely where my fingers had rested only seconds before.

I scrambled wildly back, heart pounding. A dark head emerged from between the cars as a figure climbed the ladder.

Iskander.

"No, stop!" I said—stupidly, because he couldn't even if he had wished to.

He made no reply, only drew his other knife as well. Their blades flashed in the night as he approached.

I laid frost on the knives, hoping to force him to drop them. The blades went white, but he only shifted his grip slightly, as if to get a more secure hold.

Curse it—I'd forgotten the handles were wrapped in leather.

I tried to lurch to my feet, some vague idea of outrunning him in my head. A blade whistled past my ear, and I ducked back down onto the roof. Iskander bent over me, and I caught a glimpse of his face: utterly calm and without either rage or fear.

If I died here, Christine would never forgive either of us.

I seized his wrists, striving to keep him from plunging the knives into me. But Iskander was far more athletic than I could ever dream of being. I might hold him off for a few seconds, but no more than that. I had to use magic, somehow, I had to *think*—

Energy surged into me as the train crossed the arcane line.

I grasped it, in the seconds it took to clear the line, and funneled every bit of magical fire I could through myself and into Iskander.

He screamed, back arching, but I closed my eyes and clung to him, refusing to let go. My scars ached, and I tasted metal and something burning…and then the line was beyond my grasp.

Iskander slumped to the side.

I rolled out from under him, then pulled him away from the edge of the boxcar. Blood slicked his face, trickling from his nose. Something black and dead mixed with the red.

With shaking hands, I checked for a pulse. Oh God, if I'd killed him along with the corruption…

His heartbeat met my fingers, strong and sure. Overcome with relief, I slumped over him for a moment.

I had to keep going. I had to reach Marian.

"I'm sorry, Iskander," I said aloud. If he heard me, he gave no sign. "I don't want to leave you here, but…I've no choice."

Turning away from him, I returned to the gap between cars. This time, I didn't hesitate to leap over it.

CHAPTER 38

Griffin

"WHAT IS THAT?" I asked.

Christine and I had been making our way forward, jumping from car to car. A perilous undertaking in the dark night, especially for Christine in her skirts, but it wasn't as though we had any real choice. We had to get to the front of the train and reach Marian.

And Whyborne, I hoped. If we weren't too late.

We couldn't be too late.

A dark shape lay in the center of the boxcar in front of us. I drew my pistol, then leapt the gap. Christine did the same, and we approached cautiously. Then a gasp escaped her. "Kander?"

She ran to him. I stood back, pistol at the ready…but no. I blinked, looked at him again.

"The corruption is gone," I said.

Christine knelt by him. "How?" she asked. "Why? Kander? Can you hear me?"

A groan escaped him and he blinked. "Oh, sod it all…my head."

I joined Christine. Iskander squinted at me; the whites of his eyes looked unnaturally dark in the dim light. Blood slicked his face, and he gripped Christine's hand as he sat up shakily. The wind tore at his dark hair, and he winced as the cars rattled and vibrated beneath us.

She embraced him, then kissed him fiercely. "You're all right! Well, mostly," she added. "What happened?"

"I…I'm not sure." He frowned—then a look of horror crossed his face. "Dear God! Christine, I threatened your life! I—"

"Yes, yes. You were under Marian's control," she said dismissively.

He shook his head slowly. "None of it even felt wrong," he said. "It all seemed…natural. I didn't fight against it, didn't question it. Then I tried to kill Whyborne…"

"Whyborne?" I leaned forward. "What, just now?"

He nodded. "Yes. We fought—I meant to stab him—and then something happened."

"We crossed the arcane line," I said. "He must have burned the corruption from you, just as he did from himself."

"I only know I feel as though the train ran over me." Iskander lay back, hand to his head.

Christine and I exchanged a look. "Kander's in no shape for a fight," she said. "But I'll come with you."

I shook my head. "No. Don't you remember in July, when Whyborne accidentally channeled the power of the arcane line through me? Iskander could lapse back into unconsciousness at any minute. One of us needs to stay with him."

She looked torn. "I…"

I held up my left hand. "I'm Ival's husband. I think that entitles me to claim the honor of helping him."

"You're right." Christine said. "I'll stay here with Kander, then."

"Thank you." I started to rise to my feet. The wind threatened to tear my words away, and I lifted my voice to a shout. "We're going to try and stop the train. Secure yourself and Iskander, if you can. I don't want either of you falling under the wheels."

"Excellent point." Christine held out her hand, and I shook it. "Good luck, Griffin. Send Marian straight to hell for me."

CHAPTER 39

Whyborne

MY LEGS WERE shaking badly by the time I reached the coal car.

I didn't dare look behind me, didn't dare divert my attention from my agonizingly slow progress up the length of the train. The train's speed continued to increase; they'd built a good head of steam and were putting it to use, the miles clipping past beneath the wheels, the wind tearing my hair and stinging my eyes. The landscape around us was utterly black, the sky above spangled with stars.

Where was Griffin now? And Christine?

I couldn't worry about them. Somehow I had to stop the train. My plan, such as it was, consisted of overcoming the engineer and fireman, and applying the brake. I was fairly certain I recalled which lever to pull. I was the heir to Whyborne Railroad and Industries after all; surely I could figure out how to stop one of our own locomotives.

All right. I had only to leap to the coal car, and thence directly into the cab.

I took a deep breath, tensed every muscle, and jumped.

The coal formed far shakier footing than I'd anticipated. The pile instantly began to slide beneath my feet, and I sprawled onto my back. I caught a glimpse of the lantern-lit cab, the engineer turning from the controls toward me.

Without the slightest pause, he grabbed the coal shovel with the clear intent of using it against my head.

I scrambled to my feet, or tried to—the coal kept slipping out from under me. The engineer lifted the shovel high, the edge of the blade aimed at me, and brought it down.

I rolled frantically to the side, and it bit deep into the coal, missing my fingers by inches. Undeterred, he lifted it and struck the other side, forcing me to roll in the opposite direction.

I fetched up hard against the side of the coal bin. He lifted the shovel again, and I lunged up and back, parting my legs so the edge missed my groin by the breadth of a hair.

Before he could withdraw the shovel from the coal pile, I wrapped both legs around the handle, above the blade, to keep him from pulling it free. He yanked hard, and I laid frost on the wood.

The engineer let go with a startled grunt. I reached for the wind howling past the train and snapped it around the side of the cab, magic adding to its force so it punched into him like a great fist.

I caught a glimpse of his face as he tumbled away into the darkness. God—I hoped he fell clear of the train.

If he hadn't, there was nothing to be done now. Clinging to the shovel as a prop, I managed to get to my feet and step from the coal car to the cab. Now, if I recalled correctly, the brake was—

Marian stepped out of the fireman's station.

The antler-like projections on her forehead swept the roof, and the clusters of orange tendrils on her back squirmed. Her mouth split open in a grin, revealing black mold and something *moving* deep inside her throat.

"How lovely. My meal has delivered itself," she said. "And I didn't even need to bring a dining car."

~ * ~

I acted on instinct, flinging frost and wind at Marian. To no avail: she swallowed my spells down as soon as I could form them.

"Yes," she said. "Please, continue. Weaken yourself and make me stronger."

My heart pounded. If I could just get past her to the brake—

But how difficult would it be for her to get the locomotive moving again? If the engineer had survived, she could summon him back almost immediately.

I needed to stop Marian, now, in whatever way I could.

I grabbed up the coal shovel, but she struck it from my hand before I could swing it. Both of her hands locked on my wrists, the feel of her flesh horribly smooth and spongy.

"I know what you are, little spark," she said with a grin. I fought, trying to wrest my wrists from her grasp, but she was inhumanly strong and held me with no apparent effort. "Tonight, I'm going to eat you. And in a few days' time, I'll be in Widdershins, where I can drink from the maelstrom itself. The corn will be only the first source of infection; once I have the energy of the vortex at my disposal, I'll be able to create new spores." She laughed, the earthy stench of her breath ghosting over my face. "I'll grow an empire of the infected. I'll create a world where no man is driven to his death for being different. Humanity will live in perfect harmony."

I flung my full weight against her grip, but she only laughed—and slammed me against the backhead. I struggled, the heat of the boiler soaking even through the heavy iron, but she held me pinned.

The boiler.

Marian leaned in close and began to feed.

I could feel my strength sapping almost immediately. She'd drain me, drink every scrap of arcane energy from my bones, and toss my husk away like an empty bottle. In a day or so, she'd ride triumphantly into Widdershins—hidden at first, no doubt. The infection would spread through the corn, then through her spores, until everyone and everything I'd ever loved was corrupted.

How far would it spread before she was stopped? If anyone even could stop her, with the infinite well of the maelstrom to feed from?

I ceased my ineffectual struggling and concentrated. On the other side of the heavy iron backhead, I sensed the water pumping through the boiler.

With all the remaining strength I could muster, I pushed the water away from me. Away from the fire box, to the front of the train.

Without the water, the iron of the boiler would become superheated over the fire box. Marian would drain my strength, and without my magic to hold it in place, the water would flow back. Hit the superheated metal.

Flash instantly, uncontrollably, into steam.

The explosion would probably vaporize us both. But at least Marian would be stopped.

Iskander would be saved, assuming he didn't fall off the boxcar beneath the wheels. He and Christine would have a chance, at least, of growing old together.

And Griffin…

He'd have Christine and Iskander, Father and Mother, Jack and Persephone and the Mother of Shadows. He wouldn't be alone.

A figure rose up behind Marian, an ax clutched in his hands.

"Leave my Ival alone!" Griffin shouted.

~ * ~

The sharp edge of the blade bit deep into Marian's neck, severing her head in a single stroke.

There was no blood, just a sort of wet oozing, and her body didn't fall. Still, her grip loosened, and I tore myself free.

Her arms flailed for a moment—then she crouched on the coal-black floor. The antlers had prevented her head from rolling far, and to my horror, I saw her eyes glaring at me from behind her fungal veil.

"Ival!" Griffin grabbed my arm. "Are you all right?"

"Yes—but not for long." Even without her feeding on me, my strength was fast running out. "I've affected the boiler with magic, to make it explode, but I can't keep it back for long! You have to escape!"

His eyes widened in fear, and he gripped me. "I'm not leaving you."

Marian lifted her head triumphantly and set it back on her shoulders.

Griffin's gaze slipped past her. "The tree," he said.

"What?"

The wound in Marian's neck sealed closed.

"The boundary tree by Dogleg Creek!" he shouted. "Never mind, just jump!"

He hauled me bodily from the speeding train. I glimpsed the dead, gnarled tree that stood at the outskirts of Fallow, the starry sky, and muddy water.

My magic failed.

We struck the water of the creek even as the locomotive boiler exploded.

For a moment, I knew only pain—the air driven from my lungs by impact with the creek, the blast vibrating in my bones. My feet struck the bottom, jarring one ankle, and for a moment there was nothing but darkness and water.

Griffin hauled me to the surface. As my face broke into the free air, a huge sheet of iron slammed down not ten feet from us, tons of metal tossed as though it weighed no more than a feather. The train rolled on above us, grinding rapidly to a halt as the air brakes automatically locked in place, the ruin of the locomotive trailing boiler tubes and flame. Of the cab, nothing was left but ash and fragments.

Thankfully Griffin was able to drag me to the bank; I didn't have the strength left to do it myself. We flopped onto the bank, gasping and coughing, clinging to each other all the while.

"Are you all right, my dear?" he asked, running a hand desperately over my face, my arms.

The flaming wreck gave off enough light for me to see his face. Bruised, blackened from smoke and coal dust, but alive.

"Whyborne!" Christine shouted. I glimpsed her running alongside the tracks, Iskander stumbling behind her. "Where are you?"

"Here!" Griffin called.

A moment later, she scrambled down the bank. "Are you two all right?"

My leg hurt and my back felt bruised, but I managed to nod. "Yes," I said. "Just very, very tired."

"You're utterly drained." Griffin pressed a kiss to my forehead. "Close your eyes and rest, my love. It's over. We're safe. And we're together."

"Yes," I said. I took a deep breath, all the tension uncoiling from my body for the first time in months. "We are."

CHAPTER 40

Griffin

I STOOD ON the train platform and took my last look at Fallow.

I wouldn't be coming back. Indeed, I suspected that soon there wouldn't be a town left to come back to.

When Marian died, the corrupted still human enough to function suddenly found themselves in the midst of actions that had seemed perfectly reasonable only moments before. Their memories, so far as we could tell, remained clear: of abandoning the dance and making their way to the fields, of harvesting everything left and taking it to the grain elevators, and of filling the train.

Of slick, gray-skinned creatures that had once been their neighbors. Of a monstrous thing created from the woman they'd gossiped about for years, pretending pity while cutting her deeper and deeper, until nothing remained but pain.

Several families had already packed up and left, all their belongings heaped in carts. More would follow. A few might hold out, to see if the drought ended and rains revived their fields. They would pretend nothing strange had happened; that it had all been a dream.

"I'm going to stay with Ruth for a while," Ma said.

She'd seen us to the rail station, along with Lawrence and his family. The Reynolds had gone unscathed, thanks to our warnings, though how long they could remain in Fallow with the town dying around them, I didn't know. I'd write regularly, and make sure they understood that if they needed a new home, Widdershins would welcome them.

"That's a good idea," I told her. At least Tate had paid Vernon for most of the harvest, so Ma had some money in the bank to draw from.

"Will you come and see me?" she asked.

I still didn't know what to feel, what to think about what she'd done. If it was even my place to feel or think, considering I hadn't been the victim of her malice. I'd wanted to have her back in my life so badly, but now that I knew what she'd done to Benjamin...how could I forgive that?

"Widdershins doesn't know her," Whyborne had told me. Whether he spoke only from his own anger, or from some deeper knowledge, I didn't ask. Perhaps it didn't matter.

"Would you welcome my husband if he came with me?" I asked Ma.

She didn't reply. I nodded. "You have your answer, then."

The porter stepped out of the private car. "Sir? We're due to leave in two minutes."

"Of course." I turned back to Ma. "Don't worry about me. I'm happy with my life; happier than I've ever been."

She took a deep, shaky breath. "Well. Goodbye, then, Griffin."

"Goodbye, Ma."

I watched her leave, then stepped inside the car and found my seat beside Whyborne. Christine sat by Iskander, reading to him from a journal. He had a cloth draped over his eyes, and as I took my seat, he lifted the edge to reveal an eye whose whites had gone red with burst capillaries. He'd mainly recovered from his exposure to the arcane fire, but the marks were still fading.

Whyborne held a piece of paper in his hands, a scowl on his face. "Of all the insolence," he muttered, balling it up.

"What was that?" I asked.

"A letter from our dear friend Mrs. Creigh." He handed it to me. I smoothed out the stationery and read:

Dear Dr. Whyborne,

Although you helped me stop Marian, I won't forget it was your fault she slipped my control in the first place. Nor will I forgive your destruction of the rust beneath the fallow place.
I assure you, we will meet again.

Sincerely,
Mrs. Cordelia Creigh

I passed the letter to Christine, and she snorted. "Sounds like a bunch of bluster to me," she said, crumpling it up again. "After what she did to Kander, she'd better pray I never catch sight of her again."

The train whistle shrilled, and within a minute, we were underway. The tracks east of Fallow were still blocked by wreckage. In addition to the exploded boiler, we'd set the boxcars alight, reducing the infected corn to ash and smoke. Whyborne and Niles had exchanged a series of telegrams; to say Niles wasn't pleased by the loss of an engine and the repairs needed to his rail line would be something of an understatement.

As a result of the blockage, we headed southwest to Colby, where we could again begin to make our way east and back to Widdershins.

Back to home.

"Could you pour us drinks, please?" I asked the porter, once Fallow had fallen behind us and we were on the open plains. "And leave us for a short while?"

Everyone else looked at me curiously, but the porter only nodded and did as asked. When we were alone again, I rose to my feet and held up my glass. I let my gaze linger on my companions, each one in turn. Iskander, every bit as much a brother to me as Jack. Christine, who never hesitated to charge forward in our defense, whether the enemy we faced was otherworldly or simply society itself.

And my Ival, of course. Tired lines still showed around his eyes, but the sense of pain, of a burden carried in silence since July, was gone now.

"A toast," I said, "to us. Whatever forces brought us together, we chose one another. You are my true family, and I love you all more than I can say."

We clinked glasses. "Same here," Christine said, and punched Whyborne on the arm.

"Ow! Why are you hitting me?" he demanded, rubbing at the spot.

"Because you were closer," she replied with a shrug.

Then she hugged me, and after a moment, Iskander did as well. Ival slid his arms around us all, and we stood in a knot for a long time, heads together. Just breathing, while the train hurtled on, leaving the past and all its pain behind.

The adventures of Whyborne, Griffin, and their friends will continue in Draakenwood, *coming 2017.*

SHARE YOUR EXPERIENCE

IF YOU ENJOYED this book, please consider leaving a review on the site where you purchased it, or on Goodreads.

Thank you for your support of independent authors!

END OF BOOK NOTE

THIS WAS A hard book to write.

Let me rewind. *All* of Griffin's books have been difficult. *Stormhaven* and *Hoarfrost* also gave me fits. Griffin has a lot of baggage; he's way more screwed up than Whyborne has ever been. I knew from book one on that I wanted to bring Griffin back to Kansas eventually, to reconcile with himself if not his parents. I hope I've achieved that here.

If, like Griffin, you are a true denizen of Widdershins, you can join your fellow citizens in my Facebook group, **WIDDERSHINS** Knows Its Own.

Inspiration for the fallow place came from the Devil's Tramping Ground in North Carolina. The tramping ground is a rough circle where nothing grows; local legend claims that's where the devil comes to pace every night while mulling over his nefarious plans. I've never seen the site for myself, but the images online suggest reality isn't quite as impressive as the myth.

Kansas achieved statehood as a free state only after clashes between abolitionists and slave holders earned it the moniker "Bleeding Kansas." After the civil war, it became one of the primary states where African Americans sought refuge after escaping the south (*Exodusters* by Nell Irvin Painter is a great resource for anyone looking for more information). Rural schools weren't segregated, and high schools even in cities weren't segregated until 1905. In a time when many states had or were adopting anti-miscegenation laws, interracial marriage remained legal, and has done so throughout Kansas history.

Kansas was also ahead of much of the country in the area of women's rights. Women's suffrage was considered a matter for the states, resulting in piecemeal laws where women in one state might be allowed to vote in school board elections but no others, women in the next might vote on any state-level elections, and women in the next couldn't vote at all. (If this sounds familiar, it's because it is. We've been through the same damned mess with everything from anti-miscegenation laws to modern marriage equality.) By 1901, Kansas cities had elected sixteen female mayors, and women held other local government offices as well. Additionally, Kansas women could own and inherit property, retain custody of their children, and file for divorce (by some estimates as many as 8% of marriages ended in divorce by 1900, usually for reason of abandonment).

Before beginning *Fallow*, I'd never before heard of the concept of the poor farm. In the early planning stages, I was in the midst of picking a location for my fictional town. To my delight, I was able to download a high quality scan of a 1901 atlas of Norton County, KS. As I glanced over the map, I was surprised to see one of the lots marked "Norton County Poor Farm." Clearly, this was something I had to investigate.

In general, there's a dearth of information about the poor farms, especially when compared to their urban counterparts, the workhouses. But in an era when much of the nation's population still lived in rural areas, some solution was needed to take care of the poor, disabled, or mentally unwell, and county poor farms were not at all uncommon, even if little scholarship has been done on them thus far. It was a fascinating piece of almost-forgotten history, and I was delighted to share some small part of it here.

ABOUT THE AUTHOR

JORDAN L. HAWK is a trans author from North Carolina. Childhood tales of mountain ghosts and mysterious creatures gave him a life-long love of things that go bump in the night. When he isn't writing, he brews his own beer and tries to keep the cats from destroying the house. His best-selling Whyborne & Griffin series (beginning with Widdershins) can be found in print, ebook, and audiobook.

If you're interested in receiving Jordan's newsletter and being the first to know when new books are released, please sign up at his website: http://www.jordanlhawk.com. Or join his Facebook reader group, Widdershins Knows Its Own.

Made in the USA
Las Vegas, NV
07 December 2023

82164513R00125